These

Broken

Pieces

LESLIE SAVISKY BOOKS

Other People's Words

Almost Too Late

These Broken Pieces

PRAISE FOR OTHER PEOPLE'S WORDS

"This story was a good look at what it's like to live with mental health issues and also what the survivor of a violent, traumatic event experiences while counting down the days to the release of her attacker.
It also felt true to what growing up and living in a small town would feel like. The story itself was interesting and compelled me to keep reading because I wanted to know what was going to happen. I enjoyed it and look forward to reading more by this author."

—JILL CULLEN, AUTHOR OF *FLIRTING WITH A NEW LIFE, SOULMATES, UNTIL* AND *FLIRTING WITH CELEBRITY*

"This book is a MUST read!! Shayne is very relatable with her anxiety, lies and trauma that (sadly) most women can relate to. I was fascinated about how the drama of her life unfolds. l and couldn't put the book down."

— COURTNEY S., AMAZON

"This first-time author did such an amazing job with her first book! This book almost immediately draws you in and makes you not want to put it down! The characters were all very interesting and how it pertains to everyday life, made it very easy to get drawn in. Many surprise twists along the way too, so I highly recommend this book!"

— LORI M., AMAZON

"This book! Oh my! Get it! Now! The characters... I love all of them. The author did a wonderful job with closing, yet I still wonder about them during my day! Please do a follow up to this book... I need more! It's intense, suspenseful, real, and a little bit of love mixed in...I could not have been happier with this book!"

— KAREN L., AMAZON

"It's one of those books you pick up and minutes you're into chapters. It's one that you think about throughout your day knowing you will get to that book again and your eyes pressed into those words that allows your mind to take you on a journey... definitely a good read."

— WILLIAM G., AMAZON

"Loved this book and was always looking forward to getting back into this read at the end of the day! I could easily visualize the settings and felt connected to the characters. A great first novel by Savisky!"

— DIANE O., AMAZON

"This book was amazing!! I couldn't put it down. I recommend this to anyone who struggles with daily life and anxiety; it's such a great book to relate to!"

— CLARISSA C., GOODREADS

PRAISE FOR ALMOST TOO LATE

"I absolutely loved this book! It was such a great read. I couldn't put it down! This book captured my attention from the start, and I couldn't wait to find out what happens next. Looking forward to more books by this author!"

—JENNIFER H., AMAZON

"*Almost Too Late* was a wonderful read. I read it in two days because I didn't want to put it down. Can't wait to read Leslie's other book."

— RENEE A., AMAZON

"Leslie Savisky has a writing style that has you hooked from the start. The way she introduces characters makes you want to keep reading to see how they evolve throughout the novel. You see this with Molly and many other characters in *Almost Too Late*."

—JOYCE B., AMAZON

"I absolutely loved this book, and I too couldn't put it down! This is the second book I've read by Leslie Savisky. She creates characters and scenery that you can see, smell, touch. The element of surprise is another testament to Savisky's talent. It's a real page turner, and I loved every bit of it. Congratulations to Leslie Savisky, and I can't wait for her 3rd book!"

— ERIN K., AMAZON

"*Almost Too Late* is a tale about survival and rebirth. This story intertwines the lives of a damaged niece and her doting Aunt with their past and present-day selves. It keeps you engaged with its seamless shifts between past and present, unveiling startling secrets and moral dilemmas.

Molly, the protagonist, must overcome more than your typical teenager needs to come to grips with what she had decided to do much sooner than she had carried out. The pull between good and evil carries into her adult life, leading her to deal with some of the same struggles she had as a child to finally break through at the end. Could lead to a sequel. Would recommend the read!"

— CARRIE N., AMAZON

"What a great read. I could not put the book down. The suspense was keeping me guessing what was going to happen next with Molly. Loved how it jumped back and forth in time with Molly's younger years. Leslie Savisky, you did a great job."

— SANDY L., AMAZON

"I picked this book up and couldn't put it down. I read it in one day. The plot had me wanting more."

— SHERRI L., AMAZON

PRAISE FOR THESE BROKEN PIECES

"Savisky explores the impact of loss, grief, and depression on a family, as well as the strength one can find through love. Her characters are real with the struggles and emotions most people face when visited by unexpected losses that fracture our lives and our hearts. The question becomes how to hold the broken pieces together and carry them on into life."

— LINDA RETTSTATT, AUTHOR OF OVER FIFTY NOVELS, INCLUDING THE AWARD-WINNING *LOVE, SAM* AND *LADIES IN WAITING*

"This story's not just a small-town whodunit but also a look at a family who's struggling with so many of their own broken pieces. It's crafted in such a way that it will keep you guessing until the very end."

— JILL CULLEN, AUTHOR OF *FLIRTING WITH A NEW LIFE, SOULMATES, UNTIL* AND *FLIRTING WITH CELEBRITY*

"Leslie Savisky creates vivid characters that each have a distinct and unique voice."

— CRYSTAL JOY MOONCHILD, AUTHOR OF THE INSPIRATIONAL JOURNALS *SHE IS A WILDFLOWER* AND *STARDUST & STORIES*

"Savisky truly captures the spectrum of human emotions as she tells the story of several characters going through various hardships in life. She does a tremendous job depicting accurate pictures of various mental health, grief, and loss concerns and how they can interact with one another in family dynamics. Her story has a lot of unexpected twists and turns that keep readers engaged!"

— HEATHER SCHERF LPC, AUTHOR OF *APPLES AND AVALANCHES* AND *GENERATIONAL GLOW*

These Broken Pieces

A NOVEL

LESLIE SAVISKY

These Broken Pieces

Copyright © 2024 Leslie Savisky

All rights reserved.

This is a work of fiction. Names, characters, places, conversations, and incidents are either products of the author's imagination or are used fictitiously, and any resemblance to actual events or locales or persons, living or dead, is entirely coincidental.

ISBN: 9798883148803

> *"How old would you be if you didn't know how old you are?"*

Leroy Robert "Satchel" Paige, who pitched his last major league baseball game at fifty-nine years old.

The record stands to this day.

> *And I will raise my hand up into the night time sky*
> *And count the stars that's shining in your eye*
> *And just to dig it all an' not to wonder, that's just fine*
> *And I'll be satisfied not to read in between the lines*

Sir George Ivan "Van" Morrison

"Sweet Thing" from his second album, *Astral Weeks*

To all the real Arlos

PROLOGUE
ARLO

When my daughter Kate was four years old, she had an ear infection. Kate's mother – my wife Celeste – took her to the pediatrician and Kate was prescribed an antibiotic. After a few days, Kate's pain from her ear infection seemed to be subsiding, and we thought she was on the mend. But then, with just two days left of her medication, Celeste and I noticed hives on Kate's arms. The hives spread to her chest and belly. Our daughter was having an allergic reaction to the penicillin, and it didn't take long before she developed hives over her entire body – on her legs and back, in her ears and eyelids, and on her scalp. Bumps developed on her lips; she would bite them and scream out in pain. Kate even had hives on the pads of her feet, so she could barely walk.

Watching Kate suffer was horrible, and I hated that I couldn't do much to make her feel better. She'd cry, yelling that the welts hurt and that she was itchy. It was summer and the weather was beautiful, but my little Kate was stuck in the house for a week. Through the window, she'd watched her older brother Sean playing outside, and you'd have thought that Kate's whole world ended from the look on her sweet, pitiful little face. Her mother and I were distraught; we hated seeing our little girl like that.

That was well over thirty years ago, and I still remember the whole thing, with painstaking detail.

But, if you think there's nothing worse than watching one of your children suffer, think again. Because when you become a grandparent, that love... well, it's something out of this world. I remember when I became a grandfather for the first time, Kate and her husband Reggie stopped by my house. We sat making small talk for a few minutes, then Kate handed me a card. I looked at her quizzically, because it wasn't a special occasion, not that I knew of.

"Just open it, Dad," Kate mused.

Both of them were smiling and laughing as I opened the card. The front was blank, with nothing more than a picture of the Pocono Mountains at dusk. A quote from one of Celeste's favorite authors, Elizabeth Goudge, was handwritten inside:

"The very old and the very young have something in common that makes it right that they should be left alone together.

Dawn and sunset see stars shining in a blue sky;

but morning and midday and afternoon do not, poor things."

That's how my only daughter told me she was pregnant,

and that I was going to be a grandfather. And at the time, I thought that it was a beautiful saying, but I did not grasp the full scope of those words until I held my first grandchild – a boy, Parker. Then, and only then, did I understand the meaning of my life. Sure, I'd been a decent father. I tried my best. But... I was *made* to be a grandfather. And I was, and still am, a damn good one.

We were like two peas in a pod, Parker and me. He was my buddy, and I loved spending time with him.

Roughly two years after Parker was born, Kate and Reggie had another child. My angelic granddaughter Paige was the love of my life. Those two could brighten the darkest of days. And those kids were perfect in every way. Yes, I loved my children. But I was purely and utterly devoted to my grandchildren.

When Paige was three years old, my second wife Natasha and I stayed with Kate's family while our house was being fumigated; we brought a bad case of bed bugs back from our recent trip to Florida.

Paige got very sick out of the blue. It started out one day that she was lethargic. The poor thing didn't have much energy and just seemed tired all day. Natasha and I stayed at their house longer than we anticipated, since Paige wasn't up for going to daycare. The school year was just starting back up, and Kate, who was a school nurse, wasn't able to take time off from work.

A day later, Paige started throwing up. Natasha and I were becoming concerned. Kate and Reggie were both in the medical field, so they tended to downplay illnesses because they saw so many sick people daily. They thought that maybe Paige simply had a stomach bug. It had been going around. They were used to sick kids, and it didn't really alarm them. Not at first.

But then, the convulsions started. And then the gasping for air.

It was late in the evening, almost midnight. Kate and Reggie rushed Paige to the emergency room, where she was admitted to the hospital for dehydration. I was retired by this point, and so Natasha and I stayed with Parker at their house.

Four days went by, and Paige was still in the hospital with no signs of improvement. In fact, it seemed maybe she was getting worse. Her doctors ruled out a brain tumor. It could be a possible infection, or maybe Paige ate something that she shouldn't have. But whatever it was, it wasn't due to a head injury or a severely high fever. The doctors talked of potential kidney and liver damage, and possible brain impairment. But they couldn't say exactly what the cause was. She could have ingested something toxic. Paige was put in a medically induced coma to let her brain rest and reduce swelling.

Natasha and I would take Parker to school, then Natasha would drop me off at the hospital. I'd stay all day, for hours on end, allowing Kate and Reggie to go home to shower and nap. Meanwhile, Natasha would run errands and take care of things at our home. She'd pick Parker back up from school and bring him to the hospital to visit his sister for a while. Then, the three of us would go back home when Kate and Reggie relieved us. Sean and Victor came to help out and stayed in the loft above the garage. It seemed like an ongoing, endless cycle, a routine that the family had fallen into.

And yet, it hadn't even been a week since Paige was admitted into the hospital.

Now, when I thought of those mornings and afternoons, I felt sick to my stomach. I witnessed some tragedy in my day, but nothing hurt like watching my three-year-old granddaughter lying in a hospital bed, breathing but not really alive. So tiny and pitiful and helpless.

On the fifth day of Paige's hospitalization, Natasha had gone out to Kate and Reggie's sunporch to look for Parker's school books and found Gibson, one of their four cats, dead on the wicker couch.

She phoned me at once. Natasha wondered if the two incidents were related – Paige being ill and the cat dying. But I couldn't make the connection. Not at first, at least.

If it hadn't been for the cat, Natasha and I would probably not have concluded that Paige and Gibson both ate something they shouldn't have.

And so, I started researching. It became quite an obsession for me. A friend suggested it may have been bromethalin. More commonly known as rat poison. So I studied everything I could on bromethalin over the next several days and learned that it generally takes three or four days after exposure before serious symptoms begin. And secondary poisoning could occur when an animal (like a cat) ate another animal (like a mouse) that had consumed the poison.

But that wouldn't explain Paige. Sure, she was a toddler, but the girl didn't eat a rat. It could have been an accidental ingestion, but Kate and Reggie didn't have any rat poison or anything remotely similar. No antifreeze in the garage, for example. This wasn't *Dateline*.

I discovered that, luckily, someone (even a small someone) would have to ingest a large dose of bromethalin for it to be deadly. So, more than an accidental ingestion.

Which is what the police officers said most likely occurred. A routine sweep of the neighborhood commenced, only because I contacted them. Of course, none of the neighbors knew or saw anything. It was assumed that Paige's illness and Gibson dying were purely a coincidence.

Kate and Reggie took this at face value. They were sleep deprived and naturally, not in their regular state of mind. And, after all, their little girl had survived. And surely, no one would poison a toddler and a cat on purpose, right?

Natasha and I weren't so sure. It seemed highly unlikely that Paige would have ingested bromethalin or anything similar that the cat would have also ingested. Her doctors agreed. And why didn't anyone else in the family get sick? And why weren't any of the other cats affected? Time passed, yet these questions still went unanswered. Kate begged me to let it go, so I finally did. To an extent.

I paid for all of Paige's outstanding medical bills, but I wasn't satisfied with my granddaughter simply returning home. Natasha and I sought out child therapists and discovered that there were not many willing to see children as young as Paige. Practically none, actually. Natasha, especially, never tired of researching online and calling acquaintances who may have known of a professional willing to see Paige.

Unfortunately, the two therapists (one male, one female) we found who were willing to meet with Paige were still very wet behind the ears. The male therapist wasn't yet licensed in Pennsylvania. All the same since we agreed Paige would do better with a female therapist anyway.

Kate was reluctant for Paige to go but eventually gave in and scheduled the session and allowed me to accompany them to the appointment. Kate, who never cared for my wife, did not want Natasha attending. I gave in on that point, though I wasn't happy about it.

The counselor was a rather young, skeletal woman with a neck tattoo that read "Captain" in cursive lettering. She was chewing gum and continually tapped her pen on the table beside her. Paige was pretty much in a trance by the woman's appearance and barely spoke the entire session.

Needless to say, it didn't go so well. On the drive home, I kept peeking over at Kate and waiting for her to announce, "I told you so." She never did, but the mixture of disgust and amusement on her face said it all.

Paige never went back to therapy.

CHAPTER 1
ARLO

September 18, 2019 – Wednesday

My wife left me, which apparently came as no surprise to my adult children. They never cared for Natasha, I discovered early on. That wasn't entirely true. My son Sean grew to like and respect Natasha, but Kate never did. It was understandable though, since Natasha was significantly younger than me. In fact, Natasha wasn't much older than Sean and Kate.

After their mother died, I raised Sean and Kate the best that I could by myself. I had some help from my parents (who have since passed) and my sisters. But, at the end of the day, the kids were my responsibility. And at the time, I was resentful and angry. You see, my first wife Celeste died from a ruptured brain aneurysm. We were at a cousin's wedding reception, and Celeste fell over, right there between the tables and the dance floor. She was on her way to get drinks at the bar when she went down, in front of her entire family and several friends. And in front of our children. Sean was eight years old, and Kate just six at the time.

Later, people would say to me how fast it all seemed, how Celeste just *collapsed*. But that wasn't how I saw it then, and that's not how I saw it later, in my dreams. The whole episode was in slow motion. Celeste floated to the ground, like a sheet that was tossed in the air and then let go. Like a feather. Like those colorful parachutes they use in elementary schools. My wife simply drifted to the floor and remained there crumpled, while several folks went rushing over to her side. But not me or Sean or Kate. We stood still, none of us reacting. The kids and I were frozen in place. All three of us knowing immediately that something was terribly wrong.

Celeste died almost instantly. She was just thirty-six years old.

After my son and daughter were grown up and out of the house, I finally attempted to start dating. I did okay for myself and my family, financially at least. But that led to problems when I was looking for someone to spend my time with. I was so insecure and felt women were only attracted to me because I had some money in the bank. Surely, it wouldn't be for my looks. Although my daughter and her friends said I was a catch, I didn't see it. Kate tried to fix me up with one of her friends' moms. Sean introduced me to a lady from his office. I would go on double dates with my buddies and their wives and their friends. I had a few girlfriends, however nothing long-term and nothing meaningful.

Nothing, that was, until I met Natasha. I'd been relatively single for quite a long time – approaching twenty years by then. But I had only actually been back in the dating world for five years or so. Except it was a *long* five years. Kate just graduated from nursing school and started seeing her now-husband Reggie. Sean was living in Newark and recently accepted a position at a prominent investment firm.

So my children, who were no longer children, didn't need me as much. But, I'll admit, I needed them. Or at least an *alternative*. Or a *diversion*. And sure enough, Natasha came into my life at just that right moment and quickly became both. A gorgeous, vibrant *both*.

But she was also so much more.

It was late autumn, and I was leaving the bank, after making the life-altering decision to sell my business. I was now officially a retired man, at fifty-eight years old. Not too shabby. I was dizzy with excitement, yet also anxious about telling my kids the big news. I had opted to leave them out of my decision, because I already knew how they both felt about it. Neither Sean nor Kate wanted me to sell my business, yet they weren't interested in taking over. So, I decided not to tell them what I was doing until I had already done it.

So, really, I was distracted. I got into my Explorer and, instead of backing up out of the parking space, I put my car into drive (*not reverse*) and hit the gas. I ran my SUV into the back of a brand-new Escalade. I was so embarrassed, even more so when this young, beautiful lady exited her vehicle to assess the damage.

"I'm so sorry, ma'am," I'd said, getting out of my old Ford and rushing over to her.

"Nonsense!" She flicked her wrist nonchalantly. "Nothing a little paint won't fix." She extended her hand. "I'm Natasha, not *ma'am*." She frowned playfully.

"Arlo Callan," I stated, taking her hand in mine. Her grip was soft and warm yet very strong, and I could tell immediately this woman was a force to be reckoned with. Natasha had long, dark hair and piercing brown eyes which stared back at me behind black-rimmed glasses. She was tall and slim and one of the most attractive women I'd ever laid my eyes on. I hadn't been this enamored with someone since I'd first met my wife Celeste in college.

"Please, let me give you my insurance information so we can get this squared away. Or would you rather we phone the police and –"

"Phone the police?! Oh please, Arlo." She paused, again waving her arm in the air. "Don't you dare. Now, please listen to me. I'm going through a messy divorce, and, well frankly, I have enough on my plate at the moment."

I stuffed my hands into the pockets of my jacket and tilted my head slightly. "All right..."

"Between you and me," Natasha leaned in closer to me, and I did the same. She had a tendency to do that, I would later learn. A way of bringing a person near her, physically and emotionally. Natasha made you feel like, at that moment, you were the most important person on the planet. Over the years, I would witness her do this with complete strangers and close friends alike.

"I already have two speeding tickets under my belt, and I don't want to get the insurance company involved. My soon-to-be ex-husband would have a damn field day with another fender bender, even if it wasn't my fault..." She halted, giving me a childish grin.

"Well, I need to compensate you for the damages," I

responded, feeling rather sheepish. "Do you want me to follow you to your car garage?"

Natasha hesitated before answering. She put a finger to her lips and tapped them lightly. It was a quirky habit of hers I discovered down the road. "Tell you what, Arlo. I like you," she said, as if deciding as she spoke. "Take me out to dinner – a nice place, good wine, all that – and we'll call it even."

I was slightly amused and extremely curious about this exotic woman, so I agreed. She chose the restaurant and the day and time. We met that Friday evening at seven-thirty, which was not much earlier than when I turned in for the night, I'm embarrassed to admit.

Nevertheless, Natasha and I talked for hours, which seems odd now, looking back. We couldn't have been more different, her and I. For one, she was beautiful, and I was an old schmuck.

Natasha didn't have any children, but she'd been married twice. And Natasha was young. I didn't know it then, but I was twenty-five years older than she was. Sean, my oldest, was only five years younger than Natasha; there was a seven-year difference between Kate and her. And, as one could imagine, it was a point of contention with my kids, particularly Kate.

Regardless of what my kids or anyone else thought, I fell for Natasha. Our May-December romance was a whirlwind and it moved fast. Natasha's divorce from her second husband was finalized two months after we started dating. A week later, she moved into my house. The following month, Natasha rented her house out and moved the rest of her belongings to my place. It wasn't a problem for me; I had a big place that sat on several acres, plus a sizable three-car detached garage and two sheds. And really, this place of mine, it had been too empty for too long.

After the kids moved out, it was just me for quite a while. So there was plenty of room for Natasha and all of her possessions. Strangely, I felt very comfortable with all those frilly, feminine things in my house once again. Things I didn't even know I was missing at the time, like fancy towels or jewelry on a dresser or fruity smelling shampoo in the shower. Women have a knack for making a house into a home.

I felt like I had finally been given a second chance at love, and I didn't want to lose it. Not ever. So after a wonderful seven months, Natasha and I married in a small ceremony on my property. Our property.

I enjoyed my life with Natasha, and I felt truly happy and fulfilled for the first time in a long time. We would go to dinner and dancing. We'd go on vacation – to a national park or the beach. We flew to New Orleans on a whim.

During our marriage, I became a grandfather, twice! Natasha, although still rather young, turned out to be an excellent step-grandmother. The kids called her Nooni and simply adored her. (Don't ask me where Nooni came from, I think maybe Parker couldn't say Natasha.) We'd take Parker and Paige to the playground, to the zoo, or the movies. We'd sneak the kids to McDonald's and make them promise not to tell their parents. *Hell, that's what grandparents were supposed to do, right?*

Reluctantly, Kate allowed Natasha and me to keep the kids overnight every once in a while, so she and Reggie could have a night to themselves. Of course, I'd sold my business (which had been quite lucrative) and Natasha eventually sold her home (which she got in the divorce). Natasha also had family money, and the two of us both invested well. Not only did we have the time, but we also had the money. And I was loving life again.

But, like I said at the beginning, my wife left me. Just days before our ten-year wedding anniversary, Natasha gathered up her fancy, girly things that I had grown to love so much and went to stay with her friend in the city.

CHAPTER 2
ARLO

September 22, 2019 – Sunday

It was two days after our wedding anniversary. I couldn't sleep. Four days earlier, Natasha told me, in so many words, that she didn't know if she wanted to be married anymore. She said she needed space, packed up her personal belongings, and went to stay with her best friend, Joyce, in Newark, New Jersey.

I got out of bed and went downstairs into the kitchen. Those odd green lines on the microwave read 11:45 p.m. I opened the refrigerator and grabbed a bottle of Harp Lager, which I used to take my cholesterol pill that I'd forgotten about earlier. Then, I fumbled through the drawer next to the pantry and pulled out a cigar. I had a Humidor in the den, but always kept a few of my favorite Montecristo cigars close by. Natasha never liked me to smoke in the house, so out of spite and pure defiance, I lit the Montecristo in the kitchen and leisurely made my way out onto the deck, which was just past the kitchen.

I sat outside staring into the night. My house, detached garage, and sheds sat on close to six acres. There was no one to bother me out here. My closest neighbor, Harvey, was over a half mile away. I liked it that way. Only, I was missing my wife. Why she left, I couldn't really say. We'd been getting along very well. And actually, we'd just returned home from a trip to see my older sister, Audrey, in South Carolina and had a great time.

Natasha assured me she wasn't having an affair, although I wasn't so certain. Remember now, I am a sixty-nine-year-old man. My beautiful Natasha was in her mid-forties.

I always kind of expected that she'd eventually leave me for someone much younger. But again, Natasha promised that she hadn't been unfaithful. Yet, I'd started to question the times when she'd been away for long periods of time – shopping with Joyce or another friend, Pilates class that lasted three hours. Things that I didn't think much of at the time were now coming to the forefront of my mind.

But all I could get out of Natasha was that she'd been depressed for quite a while and needed time away to think. I had noticed that she'd lost some weight and seemed depressed at times.

So I'd give her time.

Meanwhile, I'd puff on my cigar and stare into the night and miss her.

I only just lounged back in my favorite deck chair when I heard a noise. It was coming from beyond the yard in the woods. I couldn't quite describe the sound. It sounded rumbly and feral, but not like a bear. *Was it a coyote or fox? Maybe a bobcat?* I stood up to take a closer look when I saw a figure at the edge of the woods, about sixty or seventy yards away from the deck. I didn't have my glasses on, so I leaned forward and squinted, trying to get a closer look. The animal was on all fours.

The noise was louder this time. Standing up, I leaned over the railing and squinted again. The sound was more of a growl, but then there was screeching. I assumed it was, in fact, a bobcat – could it be mating season? I had no idea, but the question made me sound educated on wild animals, and I chuckled to myself. Still holding my cigar, I edged my way toward the wooden steps. Why? I didn't know, really. I didn't have my rifle on me, and not that I would have shot the damn thing anyway. My eyes finally began to adjust to the darkness.

The animal wasn't looking at me. It appeared to be hunting something behind one of the sheds.

I continued creeping down the deck, inching closer to the stairs. Still squinting and staring out into the night, like an idiot. I hadn't realized that I'd made my way over to the stairs. My next move to the right was off the first step. I lost my footing and tumbled down – the whole way down – finally landing on the concrete drive at the bottom.

For crying out loud.

My right arm was pinned underneath me, and I burned my chest with my Montecristo, which I was somehow still holding. Immediately, I ached all over.

"Son of a bitch!" I yelled out, to no one. Except the bobcat. I heard a snarl as he attacked his prey and retreated into the woods. He wasn't going to help me out, that bastard.

CHAPTER 3
ARLO

September 26, 2019 – Thursday

"Dad!" Kate called out, knocking lightly on my door. Well, her door. I was sitting at the small breakfast counter, eating wheat toast and drinking my morning coffee.

"Come in."

Kate opened the door and had that sympathetic look on her face; she wore it often around me. "How you doing, Dad?" Kate sat down on the stool next to me and patted my good arm. The right one was in a synthetic cast and sling. "Did you take your meds this morning?"

"I did."

"And last night?"

"I'm not completely incapable, you know," I retorted, behaving more like one of Kate's children than her father.

"Well, *sir*. Excuse me. I didn't mean to imply you weren't. I was just concerned. Sue me for being worried about my old man," my daughter teased. Kate got up, grabbing my coffee mug as she stood. She walked over to the other side of the small kitchen and filled my cup, then placed it back down in front of me.

"Where are the P's?"

"In the car already," she paused and nodded toward the driveway. "We're taking off. If you need anything, feel free to call me or Reggie. Anytime, okay?" Kate took the last of the creamer and dumped it into my mug. "Okay, dad?"

Kate was beautiful, like her mother had been. Both Celeste and Kate were petite and had bright green eyes and light brown, wavy hair. Kate had an animated, lively way about her, almost manic at times, which is what reminded me of Celeste most of all. Sometimes, looking at my daughter, I could almost be brought to tears. Do not get me wrong, I loved Natasha very much, But Celeste was the mother of my children, and I still missed her after all these years.

To put it simply, sometimes looking at Kate was honestly painful.

"All right. Well, since I'm not *permitted* to see my grandkids before school, please tell them we're going for ice cream when they get back."

Kate grimaced and shook her head dramatically. She shook a finger at me. "Not until after dinner. You spoil those two!"

"Grandfathers are supposed to spoil their grandkids." I put my palm out and shrugged. "It's what we do. Besides, Parker and Paige are the only ones I have. Clearly, Sean isn't having any kids."

"He could adopt."

"Yes, but he won't. Victor likes the... what's he call it?" I asked, snapping my fingers a few times.

"The nightlife," Kate said, giggling.

"Ah, yes. That's it." I paused, laughing a little too. "The *nightlife*. Victor likes to party too much. Don't get me wrong, Sean and Victor would make great parents, but I don't see any more grandkids in my future. The P's are all I have. Frankly, they're all I need."

"Well, yeah. They can be a handful, though.

I chuckled in lieu of actually verbally agreeing with her because, well... Parker and Paige could be a handful, but I didn't know if I should admit it. And because I treaded lightly when it came to Paige and her abilities.

Besides, I'm Pappy. My grandkids could do no wrong in my eyes.

My son-in-law, Reggie, was a huge baseball fan. Reggie's paternal grandfather was... *what do I say now?* African American? No, person of color. I think that's what Natasha told me to say. I was always afraid of offending someone, my old white ass was trying to get with the times. But I digress...

I loved and admired my son-in-law. Reggie was a good husband to Kate and an even better father to Parker and Paige. At times, Reggie was much easier to talk to than my own kids.

Like I said, Reggie was an avid baseball fan. His father, also being a big baseball nut, named him after the famous Reggie Jackson.

Reggie went as far as naming the kids after baseball players.

Nicknamed "The Cobra," right-fielder Dave Parker played for the Pittsburgh Pirates and the Oakland Athletics. He batted left-handed and threw right.

And Leroy "Satchel" Paige played for the Negro Leagues,

most famously the Pittsburgh Crawfords and Kansas City Monarchs. Paige was signed to the Cleveland Indians, making him the first black pitcher in the American league.

Hence, my grandchildren, Parker and Paige.

But don't get me started on baseball. My son-in-law loved the Pittsburgh Pirates, *of all teams!*

Reggie's obsession, well... it had kind of gotten out of hand. Hell, even the cats were named after baseball players: Banks, Baylor, and Gwynn. They had another cat, Gibson, but

he died.

"Speaking of Sean and Victor, don't forget they're coming to dinner tomorrow night."

"Oh, yeah, that's right. I'm kind of free *all* day. Do you want me to pick up anything from the grocery store?"

"Absolutely not! You really shouldn't even be driving. You had a *concussion*, Dad. And I don't need you trying to lift things with that bum arm of yours!" Kate uttered, throwing an arm up in the air. Then calmer, "Just try to take it easy." But then she gave me that look, one that said she knows I didn't want to 'take it easy.'

"Okay, I won't drive," I answered. But Kate tilted her head and pursed her lips as if she didn't believe me, so I kissed my fingers on my left hand and raised them up to the sky. "Promise."

Kate kissed me on the forehead. "Love you," she said, then scooted toward the door. She opened the door, exited, and then waived back at me while simultaneously shutting the door behind her. I heard her clunky tennis shoes as she raced down the steps. She shouldn't have taken the time to stop and see me, because she might have made them all late for school. But she stopped up every day this week before her and the kids left for school.

Paige was in first grade; Parker was in third. Kate was the school nurse, so she drove them to and from school every day. Honestly, Kate was way too intelligent for her position as the school nurse, although you wouldn't know it sometimes by her demeanor. With an IQ of 132, Kate was considered gifted. But she liked working at the elementary school and loved being able to watch over the kids.

Because of the hairline fracture in my arm and the concussion I suffered from my fall, Kate and Reggie suggested that I stay with them while I recovered. I tried to argue because I wanted to stay in my own home. But I was missing Natasha and being alone was getting the best of me. Also, since Kate and Reggie were both in the medical field, I agreed that maybe it was best to be around people who knew what the hell they were doing. Medically speaking, I mean.

So for the past week, I'd been staying above their garage, in the loft. It wasn't too shabby, mind you. There was a small living room, kitchenette, bedroom, and bathroom. There was a built-in bookshelf in the living room and a small linen closet next to the bathroom door. Just enough space for me to be comfortable, but also small enough that I'd be ready to head home in another week or so.

So, what's an old man to do all day while the family's gone? I could call Natasha, but I promised I'd give her space. I could phone one of my sisters, but I wasn't feeling up to all the questions. I thought about calling my long-time friend and neighbor, Harvey. A life-long bachelor who's now retired, Harvey is generally free. But I wasn't ready for a pity party.

I walked over to the sink and dumped the rest of my

coffee down the drain. The caffeine was making me jittery, especially with all this pain medicine these doctors had me on. A picture on the refrigerator that caught my attention the first night I stayed here, and I've looked at it about a dozen times a day since then. It was a photograph of the family from my birthday two years prior, not long after my granddaughter Paige had survived a pretty serious health scare.

In the photograph, we were all standing in my backyard, the sun just beginning to set in the background. It had been a hot day. Kate and Reggie were standing to my right, Reggie and me both with an arm around Kate. Parker and Paige were in front of their parents, all of them smiling. Yet somehow, Paige still has that distant look in her eyes, the one she's had since she got sick. But, regardless, the kids were smiling. My son Sean and his husband Victor were to my left. Sean has his arm around both Victor and I. Natasha wasn't in the picture because she was the one who took it. But the rest of us, my God... we looked so *happy*.

I remembered that day vividly. And – for the hundredth time – I smiled, because that's what a father and grandfather does. And I know what you're thinking. I'm a sixty-nine-year-old man with biracial children and a gay son. Yes, I get asked often, "Doesn't that bother you, Arlo?"

This was mostly by older folks my age.

I'd respond, "What? Doesn't what 'bother me?'"

"Well... your grandkids being biracial. Sean being gay."

"My son's gay?" I'd retort, feigning shock. Because what are you supposed to say when someone asks you something so unbelievably ignorant? Well, you're ignorant back.

A few years ago, I was playing eighteen holes and drinking beer with Gus, an old friend and golfing buddy. Two other guys we knew joined us and, after a few rounds, Gus started to get sloppy. After we downed a few, we were on the green and Gus turned to me and kind of chuckled.

"Hey Arlo! Man, I gotta ask you – is that son of yours still a faggot? 'Cause I know a hot bitch for him if he's still not batting for the same team."

Because I looked at this picture on the fridge. The one that shows two beautiful children with this amazing caramel-colored skin. Both are tall like their father, with green eyes like their mother. And I saw a handsome man with a wide smile that resembled his mother. And I saw that handsome man's loving spouse, who was quirky but lots of fun and occasionally got me into mischief. Because I wondered how anyone could not love them, the whole bundle of them. I loved them all so much it hurt a little. A lot, actually. It hurt a lot.

I never did fit in with the golfers at the Pocono Mountains Country Club. Although, once I retired, that's what I tried to do. Sure, I had money. Plenty of it. But still. I didn't fit in. Picture Jack Hartounian a la Caddyshack II – that was me in a nutshell.

I started my own garbage business when I was twenty-eight. *Callan Collections*. I grew it, had dozens of staff, and serviced several nearby counties. I ran the whole operation very well for over forty years; however, it was hard work. But, after Celeste died, the kids and the business were all I had. And I got tired.

I had an offer to sell it to a much bigger corporation for quite a hefty sum of money. And that's what I'd been doing the day I met Natasha – signing over the business that I'd once worked so hard to build. Not like these fucking schmucks at the country club, who were born into money and thought that continuing to be rich was an accomplishment.

Still, I tried to fit in, to belong to something. But when Gus decided it was a good idea to bring my son Sean into his racist, sexist, bigoted mouth, that wasn't something I could stomach.

I looked at Gus, this guy that I had known for well over thirty years. The guy that helped me get into the country club in the first place. I looked at him with utter disgust. Sure, my face had said it all, but my mouth wanted to elaborate. "Fuck you, Gus."

"Jesus, Arlo. Listen, man. I didn't mean to upset you…"

"No, you listen," I said, my finger in Gus's face. "Never talk about my family." I threatened and threw down my nine iron. I wanted to hurt him, but I decided to walk away instead. And so I did. I walked away from the green, the country club, and my thirty-year friendship with Gus. And never looked back. So don't accuse me of not being awake.

CHAPTER 4
ARLO

September 26, 2019 – Thursday

No, that's not right. *Woke*, I meant. Don't accuse me of not being woke. My son-in-law Victor taught me that word, but I always forgot it. Woke, awake. You knew what I meant. *Give me a break, I'm almost seventy years old.*

I realized I'd taken the picture off of the fridge and was holding it close to me. I gave it one last look then placed it back on the fridge, securing it with the magnet – a green heart with a stack of books inside.

I didn't know what to do with myself. I tried reading, but got bored. Plus it was difficult with one good arm. So I threw the book on the couch, like an angry toddler. I already ate breakfast. I didn't want to watch television. Truthfully, I didn't even know what was on TV during the day – I spent so much time outside cutting the grass or tending to my garden, I didn't have time to sit still. And now I was being forced to, and I wasn't happy about it at all.

My arm was itchy from the cast and the sling; I tried digging at it with various utensils I found in a kitchen drawer, to no avail. Finally, I decided to do something I'd been avoiding. I took my cell phone from the nightstand, sat down on the bed, and dialed Natasha. Which was difficult using only my left hand, but I managed.

The phone rang several times, and I was just about to hang up when she finally answered.

"Arlo, hello."

"Hi there." There was a long pause.

I stood up and walked out to the living room, and paced in front of the couch. I found myself circling around the coffee table.

"Arlo, love? Are you there?" Natasha asked. "Everything all right?"

"Well, no actually. That's why I was calling. I know you said you needed some space. But I... well, I just wanted to let you know I fell." I walked around the coffee table, between the table, and the couch.

"You fell? Oh my, where are you now, at the ER?"

"No," I chuckled, feeling rather embarrassed suddenly. "I actually fell a few days ago."

"What? When exactly? Wait, just a sec." I heard a muffled sound and assumed Natasha put a hand over the phone. "Okay, sorry. Joyce was calling for me. She's leaving for work. I'm here. Are you hurt?"

I walked behind the couch and realized I had been making a figure eight pattern: behind the sofa, between the couch and coffee table, in front of the table, and back around. "A little," I said, finally. "I fractured my right arm. But I'll be okay. I just wanted to let you know."

"*Fractured*... you mean broken?"

I didn't answer.

Natasha groaned. "Do you need me to come home?"

I wanted to say yes, to tell her that I needed her, and I wanted her to take care of me. And that I missed her. But I didn't. I told Natasha when she first left that I would give her space. And even though I wanted her to come home, I didn't want her to feel obligated because I was injured. "No. I'm staying at Kate and Reggie's."

That would do it, I knew. Kate had never been a fan of Natasha, which was no secret to anyone.

Most definitely Natasha. And the feeling was mutual.

There was a slight pause and then, "Oh. Well, okay then. If you think you'll be okay there..." She sounded sad.

"I will. I just wanted to let you know."

"Do you need a ride anywhere? The store, doctor's appointments?"

"I'll manage. But thank you."

"Arlo, love?"

I hesitated, half hoping that she was going to change her mind and half hoping she was going to tell me to piss off.

"Yes?"

"I'll call you tomorrow. You know, just to check in."

"I'd appreciate that. Thanks," I said, before hanging up the phone.

I wanted to say more, to tell Natasha how much I missed her. But, for whatever reason, she needed space. So that's what I'd give her.

CHAPTER 5
REGGIE

August 19, 2016 – Friday

Kate and Reggie were in the hospital cafeteria when Arlo came rushing in. He was out of breath, and Reggie could tell something was really bothering him.

Arlo said, "Natasha found Gibson dead."

Reggie was in shock, maybe because of the situation they were in with Paige, maybe not. But whatever it was, it hit him like a ton of bricks.

"Could it be related?" Arlo asked.

Reggie was puzzled. "Could what be related?"

"What?" Kate muttered, "Paige and the cat? Dad, c'mon now. Doesn't that seem a little far-fetched?"

"No, it doesn't, Kate," Arlo retorted, taking a seat beside Reggie at the table. "And, frankly, I'm surprised it doesn't concern you more."

Reggie pondered this for a moment. "If it was related, like

maybe Gibson and Paige both inhaled or ingested something... why aren't we sick? Or the other cats?"

"Because it's ridiculous to even consider that there's any correlation between the two," Kate said, looking from her father to her husband. "Reggie, those cats are all rescues. You don't know *exactly* how old any of them are or if they have any illnesses."

That wasn't true, though. Reggie was the one who took the cats to the vet. Not Kate, not ever. So, while Reggie realized his furry guys were all rescues, he still made sure they had their shots and were well taken care of.

Reluctantly, Kate gave in and agreed with her dad and husband that someone should leave the hospital and take Gibson to the veterinarian that afternoon. That someone being Reggie.

Fortunately, the vet was Reggie's second cousin and always squeezed him in. Reggie wasn't even out of the hospital parking lot before he called the office. He got the receptionist, who he may or may not have flirted with on occasion, and told her why he was calling.

Dr. Holland could see them in an hour, so he rushed home and quickly spoke with Natasha, who had wrapped poor Gibson up in a bath towel.

In the car ride to the vet, Reggie finally succumbed to tears. He hadn't cried since his pap passed away, which had been a few years ago by then. The two of them were close, and Reggie still fondly remembered watching baseball with his pap. He spent a lot of time at his grandparents' house in the summers. Reggie's grandmother would make popcorn and his pap let him drink soda, something that was forbidden in his parent's house ("Boy, you're wild enough," Reggie's mom would say).

Originally from Pittsburgh, Reggie's pap had been an avid Pirates fan, despite their generally terrible record. Shoot, they hadn't won the World Series since 1979. His pap would tell Reggie all about watching the Pirates play at Forbes Field, while his grandmother would roll her eyes and laugh.

"*Obsessed!* That's what you are!!" she'd say and giggle.

One of pap's favorite players was Willie Stargell, but the man had a true passion for the Negro Leagues players. He taught Reggie all about the players, and then sort of quizzed him when they watched baseball or ate dinner. At times, they'd walk to the local ice cream stand, just the two of them, and Reggie could get *two* scoops if he answered all of his pap's baseball trivia questions.

When Reggie and Kate (okay, Reggie, really) adopted the cats, one by one early in their marriage, Kate hadn't necessarily minded, but made it apparent that she wasn't taking care of them.

Reggie didn't know if it was an early (and bizarre) midlife crisis or the death of his pap, but rescuing the cats felt like the right thing to do. Naming them all after famous baseball players – Ernest Banks, Bob Gibson, Tony Gwynn, and Don Baylor – made him feel closer to Pap.

At the vet's office, Reggie stood across from his cousin, Andrea Holland, as she gave Gibson a once over.

"Reggie, you said it's been a few hours since Gibson passed?" Andrea asked from across the exam table.

Reggie shrugged. "I can't say for certain. We... Kate and I... have been at the hospital nonstop. But Arlo and Natasha have been staying with us. I'm sure they would have noticed Gibson. I mean, we use the sun porch all of the time to come and go," he said, unconsciously petting Gibson's belly.

Andrea gave her cousin a sad smile. "I'm so sorry to hear about Paige. I mean, God... it's not fair what you guys are going through."

She took off her latex gloves and patted Reggie's arm. He realized that he was still petting Gibson and stopped, folding his hands behind his back.

Reggie nodded. "Thanks, I appreciate it. So what do you think we should do? About the cat, I mean."

Andrea walked over to the sink, threw the gloves away, and washed her hands. "Reggie, do you want me to be completely honest with you?"

"Well, yeah. Of course."

"We don't know how long it's been since Gibson died. But the blood's most likely clotted, so it's probably too late for a blood test."

"What about other testing or surgery? To see if Gibson ate something that Paige may have eaten too. I mean, it's a possibility, right?"

Andrea returned to the table and covered Gibson with the towel once again. "Reggie, we're talking about a necropsy and –"

"A what?"

"A necropsy is an autopsy for pets. It's not something I typically do at the office, because there's a lot of moving parts. I'd have to open Gibson up, take tissue samples, send them away."

Reggie was torn. His three-year-old daughter was in a coma, and here he was thinking about a dead cat.

"But could it be worth it?"

Andrea put her palms up, as if she was figuratively weighing the options. "If it were me and I really wanted to know what happened to my pet, I'd drive him to the University of Pennsylvania for a proper necropsy. It's a veterinary teaching hospital in Philly. Or there's always Cornell in Ithaca. It's really not that costly."

Reggie needed to ask. "But if you were me, would you do that?"

She sighed and crossed her arms. "Truthfully? No, I wouldn't. Reggie, Paige *needs* you right now. Kate and Parker need you. I know you loved Gibson. And, I'm saying this as your cousin. As a veterinarian *and* a mother. Gibson is an animal. Paige is your child."

She was right. Reggie knew she was. But still. "What do you think happened to him, Andrea?" He was getting irritated. Andrea wasn't telling him what he wanted to hear.

"We don't know *exactly* how old Gibson is, but he's not a senior cat. Could have been a blood clot. Heart failure. He could have ingested something he shouldn't have. We wouldn't really know without the necropsy."

Andrea leaned back against the counter behind her. "Are you going to be okay with not knowing?

CHAPTER 6
NATASHA

September 26, 2019 – Thursday

Joyce had been my best friend since my family moved to the states. I was in second grade when my parents, sister, and I left Russia, and we all knew very little English. Joyce and I met at recess, and she kind of took me under her wing. She helped me learn the language. The two of us became inseparable, and the rest, as they say, was history.

When Joyce got dumped the day before prom, I went as her date, even though it was frowned upon back then. When she couldn't find work after college, I got her a job at my parent's company. When my mother died and I couldn't bring myself to get out of bed, Joyce would bring me donuts and coffee and just lie next to me while I cried uncontrollably.

I was at the hospital when Joyce had the twins. And also when Joyce's husband left her for his coworker that he knocked up. And I took her to Cabo when both boys went off to college and she became an empty nester. Joyce let me stay with her when I was going through my first divorce. She held my hand after each miscarriage and at my sister's funeral. My only sibling, who died much too early.

Joyce was there when I moved in with Arlo. And now, she was letting me stay with her in her apartment, until I made yet another life-altering decision. My life seemed to be in a perpetual state of limbo as of late, and Joyce let me simply just hang there. I valued her more than any other person on earth.

But, my God, was Joyce messy! One thing about living with men – you can move and manipulate your living space, so it turns into what you want. But cohabiting with another woman? *No.* And, although Joyce and I have been friends for over thirty-five years, this was her home, and I was merely a guest. Some might say an *intruder* of her personal space.

So, when Joyce was off at work or running errands, I'd secretly tidy up or toss a few old papers out here and there. But to come out and tell her I was cleaning up, well... she probably would have killed me. Once, she almost caught me. It was two days ago, and Joyce couldn't find a word search in the newspaper she'd been working on. (And who still got the newspaper? No one besides my husband, that's who.) She looked everywhere – on the kitchen counter, under the couch, in the bathroom – to no avail. I swore to her that I didn't throw it out, which was a lie. But listen, in my defense, she was never going to finish it anyway.

And slyly cleaning my best friend's apartment while she was away and then hoping she didn't notice... well, it was the only thing that kept me going these past several days. I felt like a criminal, stealing bits of junk and tossing them, in the hopes of getting away with it.

Although Joyce had been so gracious to let me stay with her, yesterday marked one week and I could tell she was starting to get, I don't know... annoyed. Or anxious maybe? Concerned? Concerned was probably the best way to describe it.

I'd been cleaning up after dinner Wednesday night when Joyce walked into the kitchen, taking plates and silverware and putting them into the dishwasher.

"Thanks for dinner, Tash," she said, nudging my arm with her elbow.

I was in the middle of washing a large pot, and some water splashed up on the counter. I eyed Joyce playfully.

"Hey, what?" she joked and put her hands up in the air.

"Just stop. You're wrecking the place!"

"Excuse me for wanting to help clean my own kitchen."

I gave her the finger, and we both laughed.

"Have you talked to Arlo?"

Ah, there it was.

I shook my head. "Not yet. And don't mother me, Joyce. I know I should call him."

Joyce turned and leaned back against the kitchen counter. She ran her fingers through her short, dark hair and then adjusted her glasses. "He is your husband, Tash. He deserves the truth... don't you think?"

I didn't answer at first. I sighed heavily, exhaling slowly. "Listen, Joyce..."

"No, no. You listen for once, Natasha." Joyce smiled, her mouth all teeth and gums. "This is coming from a place of love..."

"Oh, for fuck's sake, Joyce. I hate when you start with that 'place of love' business –"

"Natasha Petrova," Joyce began again, completely ignoring me. "I've never seen you at a loss for words before. Why now? Tell Arlo the truth. You need to talk to your husband."

CHAPTER 7
ARLO

September 26, 2019 – Thursday

It was the end of September, and unconventionally cold for that time of year. Kate and her family lived in a small town called Row Point Lake, which was in the Pocono Mountains, southeast of the Delaware Water Gap. I managed to put on my boots, which I'd left tied and awkwardly slipped out of the night before. I fought to get my jacket on for several minutes because I couldn't manage to get it over my cast. I ended up tossing the jacket on the couch and leaving the loft wearing nothing more than a t-shirt and jeans, which I struggled to button. At the bottom of the steps, which I was carefully descending, I lit my cigar and walked to the end of the drive.

Kate and Reggie's house sat to the left of the driveway. It was a split entry (oddly composed of half brick and half siding) that looked similar to most of the other houses on the street. Although, strangely, a few larger, stone houses were mixed in, as if to show the others what they were missing out on. I didn't mind where my daughter lived, and I loved visiting. It just wasn't for me. I enjoyed the privacy that my home afforded me, and the quiet that came with it. Except for the bobcat, I supposed.

I turned left and strolled down the sidewalk, stopping every so often to take in my surroundings. The mountains appeared magnificently in the background, where a wonderful mixture of green and brown leaves fought against the inevitable reds, oranges, and yellows that were already somewhat prevalent in the sky. It really was a beautiful place.

Quietly, I puffed on my Montecristo, with my left hand (which again, was tricky) and got my bearings. Eventually, I ended up near the lake located in the middle of town. There were moms and dads watching their toddlers on the spacious playground, and a few couples eating picnic lunches. Dozens of folks sat on the benches surrounding the lake – eating sandwiches, drinking fancy coffees, and scrolling through their phones – undoubtedly on their lunch breaks. I spotted a rather large and threatening no-smoking sign, so I begrudgingly bent over, snubbed out my cigar on the ground, and secured it in the pocket of my t-shirt. Then I found a bench close to the water and sat my old ass down.

I watched people coming and going, some in a rush but most of them enjoying themselves. I spent little time out here as of late, and naturally never alone. I always had Parker and Paige with me and sometimes Kate or Reggie, too. The lake was sizable, but I was still able to see the other side of it. Behind me were several restaurants and businesses, which was probably why there were so many people around on their lunch breaks. I looked down at my wrist and realized I wasn't wearing my watch. I stood up and pulled my cell phone out of the pocket of my jeans; it was almost noon. Although the sun was visible, peaking through the clouds, the wind was brutal by the lake. I silently chastised myself for not trying harder to get my jacket on.

"Is anyone sitting here?" I heard someone ask, and I looked up.

A woman stood to my right; she was a petite, pretty lady who I guessed wasn't much younger than me.

"It's all yours," I answered, trying to motion with my right arm, the sling stopping me mid-swing.

"Thank you," she answered, grinning. She then took a seat at the other end of the bench. We exchanged glances then I returned my gaze back to the water in front of me. I was thankful when, out of the corner of my eye, I saw her pull a book out of her bag and start reading. I glanced over and saw it was a book on flower gardens.

We sat in silence for several minutes when I decided it was probably time for me to be getting back. I turned and the woman looked up at me. "I'm sorry, I've been terribly rude. You allowed me to sit here, and I never introduced myself." She set her book down in between us and extended her arm. "I'm Cora."

"Arlo," I said, attempting to pivot in order to shake her hand with my left hand. Awkwardly, I tried turning and we both started to laugh.

"Again, I'm so sorry. What an idiot I am!" Cora joked, playfully hitting her palm off her forehead. "As you can see, I am kind of out of it today."

"That's okay. We all have our days," I laughed and then nodded, gesturing toward my arm.

"What happened?" Cora asked, directing her attention to my sling.

"I fell down my steps," I shrugged. "So I'm the *bigger* idiot!" I added, pointing a finger at myself. "I also burnt my chest; I was smoking a cigar when I fell."

Cora eyed me curiously, then smiled. "Serves you right," she teased, like we were old friends.

I tilted my head. "What's that?"

"For *smoking* in the first place, Arlo."

"Oh. Yes, that's what my daughter said."

"See? Smart gal." she muttered, jokingly.

"She's a nurse."

"Ah..."

There was a slight pause in the conversation until I asked, "Is it any good? The book I mean." I pointed down at the gardening book on the bench between us. "I only ask because I noticed my daughter has the same book. She doesn't have much time, so she's not much of a reader. Or a gardener, for that matter..."

Cora gave me a thoughtful look and giggled. "Yeah, it's okay, I suppose. I mean, between you and me, it was a gift from my grandchildren so that's why I'm reading it. Frankly, and not to toot my own horn, but I'm already pretty well-versed in gardening. With fruits and vegetables, of course, but flowers and shrubs mostly."

"Gotcha. I get that. I often find myself wearing lots of beads and glittery jewelry."

I waved my fingers as if I was wearing lots of rings and Cora giggled.

"Do you have a big family?" I asked, suddenly thinking there was really no hurry for me to get back.

She made a wave with her hand, as if brushing something away. "Oh, no. One daughter and three grandchildren. All girls!" Cora clapped her hands, then raised them in the air, as if her prayers for all-female offspring had been answered. "What about you, Arlo?"

"I have a son, but he doesn't have any kids. My daughter and her husband have a boy and a girl. Parker is eight, and Paige is six. They live in this neighborhood."

"Oh? That's nice," Cora responded. She looked as if she wanted to say something more, but she must have thought better of it because instead she shook her head slightly and closed her eyes for a moment.

"My husband Charlie died three years ago. Almost exactly three years ago, actually."

I wasn't sure what to say just then, so I didn't say anything. In my sixty-nine years on Earth, I learned if you didn't respond, most people would just keep on talking. Which Cora did.

"He used to come sit out here quite a bit before he got sick. He liked to watch folks out on the paddle boats. And he liked *this bench* for whatever reason. Sometimes I'd join him. But more often than not, he would come here alone. Especially after he retired."

"I'm sorry to hear that," I said, because that's what you're supposed to say. "My first wife passed away from a brain aneurysm." I paused, then added, "She was only thirty-six."

Cora put a hand over her mouth. "Oh, my. That must have been awful."

"It was. But it was quick. She didn't suffer." I began

telling Cora about Celeste and, in the back of my mind, I wondered why I couldn't shut up.

None of the significant women in my life – my daughter, my sisters, my mother, and both of my wives – would ever have accused me of being a tough nut to crack. But I also didn't go around spilling my guts to every person I met. Yet here I was, telling a complete stranger things I've only shared with a handful of people my entire life.

"What about your second wife?" Cora asked, after I was finished with my story.

I chuckled uncomfortably. "How did you know that I remarried?"

"Well, you initially said that your first wife passed away. I assume you wouldn't have called her your 'first wife' unless you had a second one," she shrugged. "Maybe a third?"

Cora smirked, revealing a small dimple on her left cheek, which was rather endearing. She really was quite an attractive woman, with her hazel eyes and soft, blonde hair, cut slightly above her shoulders. I found myself wondering what Celeste would look like now, in her late sixties, had she still been here with me.

"Yes, I did eventually remarry. Just over ten years ago."

Cora smiled. "Oh, lovely."

There was an awkward moment of silence then. And it was my turn to fill the void.

"My daughter doesn't care for her. Natasha, my wife. My son, Sean, gets along with her well now. But he wasn't fond of her at first, either."

"Really, and why's that?" Cora asked, turning toward me and swinging her arm around the back of the bench.

"She's much younger than I am. That's the main reason, I

guess," I said, scratching my chin. I realized I might have to ask Kate or Reggie to help me shave...

"Maybe your daughter is jealous. Or doesn't like that you replaced her mother?" Cora suggested, tilting her head sideways.

"Oh well, I don't know about all of that. I mean, Kate is a grown woman..."

"Kate is your daughter?"

"She is," I answered, pausing thoughtfully. "And really, I mean, it seems ridiculous, really."

"And what does Natasha think?"

"Oh, you know. Natasha's aware of how Kate feels. But I don't think she ever really worried too much about it. Natasha is a strong woman. She is pleasant enough to Kate, and gets along very well with my son-in-law. And my grandkids adore her. She gets on with my son and his husband," I paused and stood to stretch my back.

"Hmm..." Cora said, expectantly.

"Natasha's pretty close with my son-in-law, Victor. I'm sorry. I don't know why I'm telling you all of this..."

I looked down at my watch again, which I still wasn't wearing. I shook my head and laughed.

"Quarter after one," Cora said, glancing down at her own watch.

"Oh! Thanks... I better be getting back."

Cora looked up at me with her hand on her forehead, shading her eyes from the afternoon sun that glistened off the lake. "Do you live in Row Point?"

"No, I'm staying here with Kate and her family while I recover," I replied, glancing down at my arm again.

"Oh! Well, that's nice. Maybe I'll see you around?" Cora posed, wrapping her sweater tightly around her chest.

I tilted my head to the side slightly. "Maybe. I plan on staying another week or so. Although I need to make a trip back home to check on things. Get my mail. Make sure the place is still standing, you know."

"Your wife... she's not with you?"

"No," I answered flippantly. "Natasha's actually out of town visiting a friend." It wasn't necessarily a lie.

"Oh! Well that's unfortunate."

I shrugged. "Bad timing."

Cora paused, then smiled. "Well, it was nice meeting you, Arlo..."

"Callan. And likewise, Cora?"

"Barnes. Cora Barnes."

I nodded and smiled. "Take care, Cora."

"Take care, Arlo."

CHAPTER 8
NATASHA

September 26, 2019 – Thursday

I had a doctor's appointment late in the afternoon and a few errands to run, so I asked Joyce to meet me for dinner. Not surprisingly, she chose her favorite Mexican restaurant, Bonita and Bean's, which I secretly despised. The walls were decorated with piñatas, sombreros, and brightly colored paintings, all of which had a layer or two of dust. But I agreed on the place because I knew Joyce loved their enchiladas and, after all, it was my treat for Joyce letting me stay with her.

As usual, I arrived before she did and found a small booth near the window. A teenage girl with purple hair and a nose ring brought me a menu and complimentary tortilla chips. Although I shouldn't have, I ordered a margarita on the rocks while I waited for my friend. It was now dusk, and the streetlights were just starting to turn on. I looked out onto the sidewalk: Newark was a busy place. It was something that I became accustomed to in my childhood and then again during my second marriage. The rush of people, the briskness in which they walked, and how you could get lost here, if you were looking to not be found. It wasn't New York City, but it was big enough.

My life with Arlo was much simpler, and I quite enjoyed it. Sure, we vacationed often and visited family – mostly Arlo's family, as my father was the only immediate family I still had.

But, on most days when Arlo and I were home, I found myself in the garden or doing yard work right along with him. Those days – those typical, not-so-special days – were the ones I loved most. Arlo was an intelligent, financially savvy man, but what I admired most was his *kindness*. He was a gentle soul, and you could see it in the way he treated his family, his friends, and me. But especially his grandchildren.

When I first met Arlo, I was attracted to him immediately; he was tall and fit for a man his age, and he had kind eyes. I also knew he was much older than I was, and I felt that Arlo would be the type of person who would want to *care for* a woman. He wasn't the sort of man who stepped out on his wife or said hurtful things. He wasn't arrogant or belittling. And after two failed marriages, Arlo was just the kind of husband I wanted and needed.

Over the past week, I found myself missing him more and more. I wanted to go home, but I knew I couldn't. What I had to tell Arlo would break his heart and, although I knew eventually he'd find out, well...I just wasn't quite ready for him to know.

I was halfway through my margarita when I saw Joyce. *Finally.* She was dressed in her traditional pale blue scrubs. I raised a hand, and she waved then held up a finger. I realized she ran into someone she knew. She was talking to an elderly couple. Joyce was animated, waving her arm and then putting both hands on the woman's shoulders affectionately. I shut my eyes and rubbed my face, silently praying she didn't invite the couple to join us. Joyce was like that, overly friendly.

When I opened my eyes, Joyce was sitting across from me, her chin resting on her folded fingers.

"Holy shit!" I screeched loudly.

A few customers looked our way, while Joyce and I offered apologetic smiles and giggled.

"Sorry, Tash. I didn't mean to scare you."

I placed a hand over my heart. "You scared the shit out of me, for crying out loud. Don't you go sneaking up on people like that," I chastised, only half-jokingly.

"I didn't sneak up on you. Your eyes were shut!" Joyce reached over and playfully smacked me on the arm. "How many of those have you had?" she asked, eyeing my drink.

"Just the one," I replied, raising my glass and taking another sip.

A moment later Purple Hair drifted over to take our order. "I'll have a mango margarita and chicken enchiladas with extra sour cream please," Joyce said, never even bothering to look at the menu. "And she'll have another margarita," she added, looking over at me.

"That's all," I said. "Thank you."

Apparently, Purple Hair was not okay with this. "You're not ordering?" she scratched her scalp with the pen.

"I'm fine. Just the tortilla chips and the tequila."

Our waitress rolled her eyes and shrugged. "Okay," she

said, then turned her attention to Joyce, "I'll put your order right in." She sighed and ambled off.

"Well, isn't she just a ray of sunshine," I smirked, shaking my head.

"Tash, you really should eat something," Joyce stated, giving me her best motherly scolding.

"I'm fine," I said, grabbing a chip from the bowl between us and nibbling it. "I haven't had much of an appetite lately."

"Fair enough."

"How was work?" I questioned, in desperate need for a change of subject.

"Okay," she shrugged. "I've been seeing so many elderly people lately. That was actually one of my clients I was talking to at the door," Joyce nodded, gesturing to the front of the restaurant, as if the couple were still standing there. "Oh, forget I told you that. Privacy, HIPAA, you know..."

I smiled and put my hands up in defense, teasing her. "Won't say a word."

I cautiously munched on another chip. In all honesty, I was starving but could barely keep anything down these days. And I hated the food at Bonita and Bean's. All I could picture were large rodents running rampant through the kitchen.

"I got a new patient today. A young girl. Sixteen, I think. She was in a pretty bad car accident. Had to give up swimming. Which, according to her mother, was her *whole world*."

Joyce was a physical therapist and was used to dealing with injuries of all kinds. She was amazing with all of her patients. Teenagers were tough for her to work with;

although she was very good with them. She wouldn't admit to it, but I had seen it firsthand.

"Not unlike you," I said, slowly and with compassion.

Joyce hesitated, considering. "Yeah. Funny thing, that."

I tilted my head a bit. "What is? The irony?"

She waved a hand in the air nonchalantly, brushing away the thought. "My accident was careless. Plus, this girl – the new patient – was really quite good, apparently. According to her mom, she was training for the Olympics," Joyce stopped. She coughed out a laugh and shook her head. "I was never that good."

"No, but you could have had a scholarship," I retorted, pointing a finger at her. Joyce broke her arm in a skiing accident our junior year of high school. She was an excellent softball player, a pitcher. She never played again after recovering from her injuries. I know it's something that's always nagged at Joyce since then, how far could she have gone.

Purple Hair brought our margaritas, setting the wrong ones down in front of us. "Food'll be right out," she murmured, turning on her heels.

"Oh, this chick is not getting a tip," I joked after the waitress was out of earshot. I swapped my drink for Joyce's.

Joyce took a sip of her mango margarita and then licked her lips. "Give the girl a break, Tash. *We* were young once too."

"Okay, but *I* was never that bitchy."

"No, no. You're right," Joyce said, putting her palms up defensively.

"See!" I laughed, waving a finger at my friend, while I sipped my drink.

"You were worse!"

I grinned. "What?! No!"

"Yes, intolerable!"

We were laughing hysterically when the waitress brought Joyce's enchiladas. She gave us both a funny look and walked away.

"You're right," Joyce said, nodding as she took a bite. "She's not a good waitress. I swear I asked for extra sour cream!" Joyce let out a long sigh and shrugged, as if this was the most put out she had ever been in her life.

"You did," I laughed, and as Joyce was digging into her food, I added, "Arlo called me today."

My friend looked up from her plate and smiled. "Yeah?"

"That's actually who I was talking to when you were leaving for work earlier..."

"And?"

I could feel myself beginning to get that hot feeling on my face, the one right before I started to cry, so I tightened my jaw and shrugged.

"Aww, babe!" Joyce muttered, reaching across the table to squeeze my arm. "What happened? What did he say?"

It took me a moment to compose myself. "He fell. Down the outside steps –"

"Oh, my!" Joyce unconsciously covered her mouth with both hands. "Is Arlo okay? I hope he's alright."

One thing you have to understand about Joyce is that she has been there for everything – every death, every loss, every man. Arlo was my third husband, and Joyce's favorite. Not only of my spouses, but of any man I'd ever encountered. She *adored* Arlo. The fact that we were apart, even if it was potentially temporary, troubled her just as much as it bothered me. Or at least, pretty damn close.

I rubbed my forehead. "I don't know, honestly. He didn't tell me much, and I suspect there's much more to the story than he's telling me."

"Mmm."

Purple Hair brought our check, and I quickly produced my credit card, handing it over to her without looking at the bill, but secretly hoping she didn't overcharge us. She took Joyce's plate and the empty basket of chips, uttering, "I'll be back in a second with your receipt."

After the waitress was gone, I said, "I can tell there's probably a lot he's not telling me."

"Uh-huh." Joyce said, finishing off her margarita.

"What?"

"Nothing. Just the hypocrisy, that's all."

I smiled. *Boy, she was good.* "Oh, I see. Because I'm not telling Arlo the whole truth."

"Bullseye, bitch," Joyce said, grinning.

"Okay you got me there. Come on. I'll get my card and let's get the hell out of here."

CHAPTER 9
KATE

September 27, 2019 – Friday

"My last patient canceled, but I need to stop by the office before heading home. Do you need me to pick anything up?" Reggie asked earlier on the phone when Kate called him on her lunch break.

Such a good husband.

"No. I think I have everything I need," she replied.

Kate could hear Reggie silently contemplating his next move. "Are you sure? Really, babe, it's no trouble."

Kate rolled her eyes and pressed her lips together tightly. "Thanks, but I picked up everything I needed last night, remember? When you and my dad took the kids for ice cream."

"Oh! Speaking of that... babe, you would have lost it! Did you know that your dad met Cora at the lake yesterday? He talked about it the entire walk there. On the way home, Paige finally said, 'Pap, can you please stop talking about Mrs. Barnes and talk about me now.' It was hysterical!"

Kate made a face. She kept her distance from their neighbor, Cora. "Oh, poor Dad! Paige has no filter."

"I don't think Arlo even knows how close she lives to us," Reggie laughed.

Ever since Cora's husband Charlie died, Reggie joked about wanting to set Arlo up with Cora. Kate assumed it was because Reggie knew Kate couldn't stand Natasha.

But Cora was kind of a stick in the mud. She lived behind them and down two houses, so their backyards didn't butt up against each other. But they were close, nonetheless.

Close enough that sometimes, when Parker and the other boys in the neighborhood played catch, their ball would go sailing into Cora's backyard and it was a whole thing...

Of course, Arlo was *still* married to Natasha. But at least Cora and Kate's dad were around the same age.

"Kate?" Reggie uttered, bringing Kate back to their conversation.

"Oh, sorry. No, I don't think they ever met..."

Reggie laughed. "Here I was trying to secretly find a way to play matchmaker, then Arlo goes and meets Cora on his own!"

Reggie was always trying to play matchmaker. He was a lover not a fighter, that's what he'd say, albeit jokingly, to Kate when they were dating.

Kate went to respond when the school secretary popped her head into her office. Even though the door was half shut, Ms. Simpson gripped it with an old, wrinkly hand and swung it open. The woman did not know the meaning of the word privacy.

"Everything okay in here, Nurse Beckford?" she asked. Kate thought that Ms. Simpson looked more like an old school marm from an all-girl boarding school than she did a present-day elementary school secretary. She wore her dark, graying hair in a tight up-do, dark-rimmed eyeglasses, and a shawl, even when the weather was warm.

Always with the damn shawl, Kate mused to herself. *The woman was so odd.*

Ms. Simpson always had a frown and pursed lips, always appearing like she just smelled something awful. And, ironically, Ms. Simpson hated children, yet she chose to work in an elementary school.

Kate covered the phone with both hands. "Just fine, Ms. Simpson. Just talking to my husband on my lunch break." Kate made a point of looking up at the old clock on the wall. "Well, I have to start hearing tests in about ten minutes, so if you don't mind..."

Ms. Simpson stared at her for a moment as if she was going to say something else, but then must have thought better of it. After a moment, she responded, "I'll leave you to it, then. Good day, Nurse Beckford."

Kate smiled and nodded. "Goodbye," she replied, then turned her attention back to the phone. Ms. Simpson turned and briskly walked away, never bothering to close Kate's door. Kate swiveled on her chair and gave the door the middle finger.

"Sorry, Reggie, Simpson just popped her head in here. I gotta run. The kiddos will be coming in soon."

Kate stood from her tiny desk in the corner. She took a drink from her water bottle and checked her face in the mirror. She didn't like what she saw. *Maybe I should get Botox,* she considered. She made a mental note to pick up more moisturizer. The nice, expensive kind.

"Okay. Well, if you think of anything throughout the day, just text me."

"Will do. But really, think I have everything I need. Love you lots."

"Love you," Reggie said then hung up.

On the drive home from school with Parker and Paige, Kate realized that she did not, indeed, have everything she needed for dinner. But Reggie would likely be home by now and, even though he offered and even though she was annoyed with him, Kate hated to ask Reggie to run back out. And she didn't want to appear like she didn't have it together, even to her husband.

And Kate still didn't trust her dad to drive, not with the concussion and broken arm.

Sean and Victor were coming for dinner. Including Arlo, that made five adults and two kids. She had enough seafood; she bought shrimp and salmon after work the day before. Parker loved seafood but Paige wouldn't touch it. Kate would make her mac and cheese or chicken nuggets, which was about all Paige ate besides fruit and ice cream. Kate baked homemade bread last night and bought vodka so Victor could make his *fabulous* Moscow Mules. She planned to make a salad and cook pasta tonight. But she forgot to buy salad dressing; her dad loved French, even though no one else did. Plus she needed lime juice for the Mules and her dad's favorite beer.

Damn it, Kate uttered under her breath.

She was *always* messing up. Always making mistakes.

Always so forgetful.

Kate had wished she was like other moms she knew. Always so fresh-faced, so put-together.

Part of Kate found those women sickening. The other part of her was mad with jealousy.

Her judgment had been cloudy lately. Too much on her mind.

"Mom, are you okay?" Parker asked from the back seat.

Using the mirror on the visor, Kate looked at her kiddos in the back seat. Funny, watching them watching her.

"Yes, buddy. It's just that Mommy forgot to pick up a few things from the store for tonight."

Parker asked, "Do we need to stop at the store?"

"Yes, but I can run in really fast. You two could probably sit in the car; I won't be long. Do you think you guys are big enough to do that for me?" Kate asked, in a sing-song voice.

"Sure, Mom!" Parker answered proudly.

"Great, thanks, buddy. Paige?"

Kate snuck a peak in the mirror again. Paige was looking out the window. Despite her height, Paige looked so small in her car seat. It almost appeared to swallow her up. "Paige, did you hear me?"

"Huh?" she asked, turning her attention back inside the car, but her focus was still not on Kate. Ever since Paige's illness, she had what was referred to as "lingering effects" – attention issues and cognitive delays being the most apparent. She also still wet the bed sometimes.

Kate turned her Toyota Sienna into the parking lot of the

grocery store. "Paige, can you sit in the car with your brother and be good while I run inside for a minute?"

"I wanna go in!" Paige insisted, scowling.

Pulling into a space near the front of the store, she turned off the van and turned around. "Paige, I'll be like five minutes. Can't you just wait here with Parker?"

"No, I wanna come with you!" she repeated, this time hitting her fist off of the door for dramatics.

Kate sat for a moment, rubbing her hands over her face. *Did parenting ever get any easier?* She didn't want to give in, but she'd been down this road before. If she got out of the car and left Paige with Parker, she'd inevitably come running in after Kate and there'd be a meltdown.

"Come on," Kate groaned. "Parker, you coming, bud?"

"Yep!" Parker unhooked his seatbelt and helped his sister with hers.

Twenty minutes later they were back in the van and driving home – salad dressing, lime juice and Harp Lager in tow.

CHAPTER 10
ARLO

September 27, 2019 – Friday

Natasha called in the morning to check on me. And, as badly as I wanted to see my wife right then and there, I told her that I was fine. Kate, Reggie, and the grandkids were taking good care of their old man.

"Oh, I see. Well, I wanted to make sure you didn't need anything during the day while you were by yourself."

I found myself pacing back and forth in front of the couch again, awkwardly holding the phone in my left hand.

"I go back to the doctors next week. They may be able to remove the synthetic cast and put my arm in a brace," I paused, sitting down on a kitchen stool. "I could probably use a ride to that."

"Oh! Sure I should be able to, love. What day?"

"It's this upcoming Wednesday. The second, I believe," I started to put my boots on, slipping into them with slightly more ease than the day before.

There was a pause, and I imagined Natasha mentally reviewing her calendar. "I can take you. What time is your appointment?" she asked.

"I have to be there at ten. Kate said she can take the day off and drive me. But if you don't mind taking me, it's up to you if you want to... given the circumstances."

"No, of course I don't mind taking my husband to his doctor appointment. You tell Kate I will pick you up. No need for her to take off work."

We left it at that, and Natasha agreed to call me Tuesday afternoon to confirm the time. So that was that. Apparently, I wouldn't hear from Natasha until then. Maybe if I fell down the steps again and broke my other arm, she'd come home for good.

I left my temporary apartment above the garage and strolled across the driveway. I let myself into the house, which was usually locked, but Kate left it open since I was staying with them. I went in through the sun porch and was immediately assaulted by Banks, their fat, gray cat. Banks was the fattest, and most likely the oldest, of their three cats. He spent a lot of time lounging in the sun. But the chubby thing still liked to eat and followed me into the kitchen to see if his begging would pay off.

It did. I opened the fridge because I was in desperate need of cream for my coffee. I pulled out a slice of cheese and broke off small pieces, tossing them down one by one to old Banks. (Reggie would have been mad, me feeding Banks like this.) He meowed at me angrily, as if I couldn't feed him fast enough. Soon, Banks had competition when the other two cats, Baylor and Gwynn, strolled around the corner to see what all the fuss was about. *I deserve a reward for remem-*

bering all of these pets' names, I thought to myself and chuckled.

"Okay, okay! Here you go, guys," I laughed.

Making sure to equally divide the pieces between the three felines, I flung the rest of the cheese on the ground in three small piles. I swear these cats would eat anything. I could have given them broccoli and they probably would have eaten it. After devouring his share, Banks turned to head back out to the sun porch. Apparently, he didn't seem to care for my lack of favoritism toward him. Baylor and Gwynn dove for the rest of the cheese.

I couldn't find any creamer in the fridge, so I decided to walk to the diner in town. I was sure the coffee was better than the cheap stuff Kate kept in the garage apartment anyway. Making sure to lock up before heading out, I left the way I came in and started walking down the sidewalk. I thought better of it and hurried back up the garage steps to get my jacket.

After five minutes of struggling to get my jacket on and then another few minutes of using the facilities, I finally headed down the road, zipping up my coat as I went. I thought about Natasha and our phone calls. I missed her terribly, and I wished that I was back home with her. I loved Kate and her family, and I enjoyed being around my grandkids, but I also wanted to be at my own home with my wife. And she was giving me mixed signals, moving out but offering to take me to my doctor's appointment. Was it over between us or did she want to reconcile?

Last night, after Reggie and I had gotten back from taking the kids for ice cream, Kate suggested possibilities for Natasha leaving. The most obvious being, in Kate's mind, was that Natasha was having an affair. She didn't come out and say quite that, but she definitely alluded to it.

"Don't be surprised if she asks for a divorce," Kate muttered.

I wasn't so sure, but then I couldn't say she wasn't. Natasha and I had been married for ten years, and I never once thought she was seeing someone else. Not once. And then, out of nowhere, she up and left, staying in Newark with Joyce and leaving me all alone. It was almost worse than when I lost Celeste – because my first wife hadn't chosen to leave me, she was just gone one day.

After a ten-minute walk, I was nearing the diner. The morning started out cloudy, but I could see the sun peeking out through some low clouds. I willed the sun to come out. I couldn't deal with another overcast day. In fact, now that I thought about it, yesterday had been the first sunny (albeit chilly) day since my tumble down the stairs. The same day I talked to Natasha and the same day I met Cora at the lake. I wondered if there was any significance to that or if my pain meds were making me nuts. I shrugged; it could be either, or both.

I opened the door to the tritely named Row Point Lake Diner, the dark green letters chipping from the glass front. I walked up to the counter and took a seat; there were several to choose from. A scattering of old timers like me seemed to be the main clientele. Not surprisingly, of course, since most kids were at school and adults were at work mid-morning on a weekday.

"Whatcha having, hon?" A middle-aged woman with bright red hair said, as she strolled over to me. She was short and curvy with a name tag that read Lola.

"Just a coffee, please."

She nodded. "Cream and sugar?"

"Both," I said, setting my right arm on the counter.

Lola peered down at my arm and frowned. "Need a menu?" she asked politely, setting a napkin and spoon down in front of me.

"No, thanks," I answered. Someone coughed loudly by the door, and subconsciously I turned my attention that way. Across the street, I could just make out the playground near the lake from where I sat.

A moment later Lola returned with a hot mug. "On second thought," I started, "can I get this to-go?"

Lola exhaled heavily, but must have decided to be civil when she saw me struggling to open my wallet with one good hand. "No problem, hon." She turned around and grabbed a Styrofoam cup and lid from behind her. Carefully, she poured the coffee from my mug into the to-go cup. Then, Lola picked up the sugar and started to pour it in, as well.

"Say when."

"When," I replied after a second or so.

She repeated this with the creamer.

"I appreciate it, Lola," I said, setting a ten-dollar bill on the counter.

She smiled appreciatively. "What happened to your arm?"

I shrugged. "Took a tumble down my steps."

"Well, you take care of yourself," Lola replied, securing the plastic lid onto my cup and handing it to me.

"Will do. Have a good day now." I nodded and smiled, taking the cup from her and walking toward the door.

CHAPTER 11
ARLO

September 27, 2019 – Friday

Coffee in hand, I headed toward the benches by the lake. It didn't take me long to spot Cora; she was sitting on the same bench as yesterday. Cora was wearing a thick wool sweater and matching hat, and she kind of reminded me of a child all bundled up like that. I laughed to myself.

"Well, if it isn't Arlo Callan?" Cora stated, making a grand gesture with her arms as I took a seat next to her on the bench.

I set up my Styrofoam cup on the ground. "Cora, a pleasure..." I said, twirling my left hand as if greeting royalty.

"You have a coat on today."

"Yes, I do. And it was a struggle getting it on, let me tell you!"

"I can only imagine." Cora shook her head. "You know, I've never broken a bone. Not once. Can you believe that?"

"No, I can't," I laughed. "I played football growing up, so

I've broken quite a few bones. And my younger sister Faye punched me in the face once when I was in high school. Broke my damn nose."

"Oh, my! She sounds like one tough cookie."

"She was. I think she was only fourteen at the time."

Cora picked up her thermos and took a drink. "Well, did she at least have a good reason for hitting you?"

I thought for a moment. "No, she didn't, as a matter of fact!" I said, feigning disgust. "There was this kid in class with me, Donny something-or-other. He was the quarterback. Parents were rich, he liked to flaunt the fact that his family had money. Cocky bastard. A real ass, you know?" I stopped and looked at Cora, who nodded.

"Well, Donny was a senior. Eighteen, like me. He liked Faye and asked her out. I found out and flipped my lid. I told him to leave my sister alone..."

"Oh!" Cora giggled. "And Faye punched you?"

"She did!" I shouted, rolling my eyes. "Donny told Faye what I said to him. Faye got upset and told me that she liked Donny and that it was 'none of my business' who she dated. Well, I can tell you one thing, that Donny was a dipshit. Plus, he was too old for her."

"Hmmm. He does seem like a dipshit."

I leaned over and picked up my cup. "He was," I concurred, taking a long drink before setting it back down. My coffee had the perfect amount of cream and sugar. *Thank you, Lola!*

"You know, come to think of it... I don't think I ever met a Donny that I liked."

I slapped my knee. "Me neither!"

Well, don't leave me in suspense. What happened – did they ever go on that date?"

"Oh, well... my parents found out and they put a stop to it immediately. They said Donny was too old for their daughter."

Cora turned toward me and wrapped her sweater tightly around her waist. "Sounds like you did her a favor then. Whatever happened to poor Donny?"

I turned my head and gazed out over the lake for a moment. "Two years later, Donny was in a car accident. He was drunk. Killed the passenger. His girlfriend I think she was." I turned and looked at Cora. "He hit another car head on. Mom, dad, and three kids. They all died..."

We sat looking at each other for a moment. "And Donny? Let me guess, he lived."

I nodded, "He lived. Spent a few decades in prison. I lost track of him after that."

Cora looked at me and grimaced. "Hmm."

"Yeah," I shrugged.

I sat silently watching Cora for a moment; she was looking out over the lake now, too. She snickered suddenly. "You know, Arlo, you really know how to get a party started!"

We both laughed hard, and Cora slapped my knee. She snorted, which I found quite endearing.

I sighed slowly. There were a few moments of awkward silence. Then, I noted the gardening book on the bench beside Cora. It was the same one that she'd been reading the day before. "You do a lot of gardening?"

I caught her lost in thought. "Oh!" she muttered, startled. "Yes! I do, actually. Not this time of year, of course. But I like to think about what I want to plant in the springtime... flowers, sometimes a few vegetables or strawberries. I order seeds a few months in advance when they're available. But most of my shrubs and plants are perennials and well-established. So, mostly I just weed and keep the garden tidy, you know."

"That's very impressive. I have a garden, too. But I'm not really that into it. I grow easy stuff. Onions, peppers, tomatoes – things that don't need that much attention. No flowers. I'm sure I'd kill them all," I chuckled.

"I'm sure you're better than you think. I have always had quite a nice garden, but after my husband died, I got more interested in it. It's kind of become an obsession, to be honest."

Cora giggled, but there was a hint of unease in her voice.

"Well, I better get going. My daughter and her family are visiting this afternoon."

Cora stood up, and I did the same. "Well, it was nice to run into you again, Cora."

"Likewise, Arlo. Enjoy the rest of your day," she said, patting my shoulder.

She started to walk away, and I waved, "Enjoy those granddaughters of yours."

Cora smiled. "You don't have to tell me twice! I already made brownies and two dozen cookies early this morning. Take care, Arlo."

"Take care." I took a seat on the bench again.

I sat there drinking my coffee and watching the people go by, wishing the sun would come out from the clouds.

CHAPTER 12
KATE

September 27, 2019 – Friday

Sean and Victor were early, of course, because they were early for everything. Not Sean's choice, though. *Victor was the one always ready to go, go, go,* Kate knew.

But this was obnoxiously early, even by Victor's standards. Kate hadn't finished setting the table, and she didn't even have a chance to fix her face yet.

"You look beautiful, as always," Reggie whispered, when he noticed her aggravation. Kate rolled her eyes.

He knew her too well. *How did he always know what she was thinking?*

"Uncle Sean! Uncle Vic!" Parker yelled, running down the stairs.

Parker trotted into the living room and gave Sean a quick hug. Sean was tall, like their dad, with bright blue eyes to match.

"Hey, kiddo," Sean said. "Lookin' good."

"Thanks, Uncle Sean!"

Victor was average height and soft around the middle. He had wild hair that was always *cool messy* and dark-rimmed glasses. Victor attempted to pick Parker up, but only lifted him a few inches off the ground.

"Oh no, not this time, buddy. You've gotten too big!" Victor screeched, rubbing his back and twisting his face. "Oof! Sorry, Parker," he added, giving the boy a fist pump.

"It's cool, Uncle Vic. I've been playing basketball," Parker beamed. He pushed up the sleeve of his t-shirt and made a muscle, which made Kate grin. "I started lifting weights."

"Light weights," Reggie added.

"*Very* light weights," she chimed in, still smiling. *My sweet, strong boy*, she beamed.

Sean gasped dramatically, then put a hand on his hip.

Victor clapped his hands together. "Wow! Would you check out those guns, Sean?"

Kate's brother folded his arms in front of his chest and shook his head. "Boy's got muscles, that's for sure. Your dad must be pretty upset you're into basketball. You know, 'cause of the whole *Pirates* thing?" Sean laughed.

"Oh, you know it!" Parker said, relishing in all the attention.

Kate laughed and threw her husband a look. Sean and Victor were endlessly teasing Reggie for his obsession with baseball.

"Sorry, Reggie. They can't all be Roberto Clementine..." Victor caught Parker's attention and winked.

Reggie, who was helping Kate set out the silverware, shook his head. "It's Clemente, Victor. Roberto *Clemente!*"

Sean, Victor, Parker and Kate burst out laughing – Reggie was obviously unaware that Victor was messing with him.

"Reggie, please forgive Victor. He's gay, you know? He knows very little about sports." Sean looked at Victor and frowned. "Poor, simple man." He patted Victor on the head.

Reggie looked up and smirked. "You guys are all jerks, you know that?" He chuckled.

Arlo walked into the dining room and looked around, smiling. "What's going on in here? Reggie, is my other son-in-law joshing you again?"

Victor shrieked and put his hands over his heart, "Papa! I would never make fun of your *second-favorite-son-in-law*!" Victor put his arm around Arlo, and Arlo patted him affectionately on the back.

Arlo then gave Sean a hug, "Love you, bud."

"Love you, Dad. How's the arm?" Sean asked.

"Meh," Arlo answered, turning his palm up. "I'm getting by. Kate and Reggie and the kids have been a huge help."

Kate dug her fingernails into the palms of her hands. She wanted to make a comment about her absent stepmother but thought better of it. "Come on, guys, have a seat," Kate said. "Parker, go find your sister."

"Okay, Mom," he replied and took off up the stairs.

While Arlo and Sean chatted, Victor started to help Reggie with the place settings. Typically, Kate preferred to do it herself, but she still needed a few moments to herself.

"I'll be back in a few minutes," Kate said to no one in particular, then headed upstairs. Parker and Paige passed Kate in the hallway, and she gave them both a pat on the top of the head before they headed downstairs. *Her sweet, sweet angels.*

Kate went into her bedroom and shut and locked the door. She sat down at the vanity and applied blush to her cheeks and concealer under her eyes. She brushed powder over her entire face and a little bit of mascara and lipstick. Kate didn't have time to do much with her hair, so she put it in a quick side braid.

That would have to do.

She opened the bottom drawer of her vanity where she kept her extra bottles of lotions and face cream, nail polish remover, and makeup brushes. In the back was a small, copper colored bottle. Kate kept her meds in the back, knowing the kids would never find them there, nor would Reggie ever bother to look in the drawer. Kate opened it up and took out two pills, medicine she'd been prescribed by her family doctor for stress and anxiety.

Kate wasn't even in her forties yet, but she surely felt like it. And definitely looked it, she thought, looking at her reflection in the mirror. Her eyelids drooped, and she noticed a new wrinkle on her forehead just the other day. And Kate needed to get back to the gym. She wished she had the money for plastic surgery. Her friend Marcy got lip filler and Botox injections, but Reggie would kill her if she did that. Reggie didn't approve of getting work done, and Kate already knew he'd say she looked beautiful the way she was. It would be a lie, but that's what he'd say anyway.

And it wasn't easy when you had to compare yourself to your stepmother, who wasn't much older than you and was, frankly, gorgeous. Yes, Kate may not have fancied Natasha, but Kate still had to admit that Natasha was beautiful. Although she would never, ever have admitted that out loud, not to anyone. But Natasha was perfect in that careless, carefree natural way that other women (well, at least Kate) hated other women for.

Her mother had been beautiful, too. Kate was a couple of years older now than Celeste had been when she died. But not only was her mother beautiful, Celeste was loving and kind and smart. Smarter than Kate. She didn't remember her that much anymore, being so young when her mother passed away. True memories melded with stories from her father and brother, other relatives and friends.

Regardless, she missed her mom.

Kate placed the pills on her tongue and swallowed them with water from the bathroom sink. After using the bathroom and washing up, she made her way back downstairs, where Sean was playing cards with Parker on the living room floor.

"Where's Paige?"

Sean sat up and looked around the room. Parker, his head still down, muttered, "Think she's in with dad."

Kate peeked her head into the dining room, where Reggie, Arlo, and Victor were seated around the table. Arlo had already started drinking, and someone brought in the cheese tray that Kate had stored in the kitchen for safe keeping.

"Hey Reggie, can you help me with dinner?"

"Sure, hon," he answered and followed her into the kitchen.

"Hey, where's Paige?" she asked when they rounded the corner.

Reggie shrugged. "I figured she was with Parker and Sean."

"Well, she's not," Kate retorted, angrier than she meant for it to come out. "I'll go look for her. I don't want to make a scene. Can you get the salad out and have Parker wash his hands for dinner?"

"Make a scene? Kate, babe... we're in our own house. She has to be here somewhere."

She gave her husband that look – the look that she gave him every so often since the incident. The look that said, *Don't fuck with me, I am this girl's mother.*

Kate almost lost her little girl once, and she would not let anyone tell her she coddled or hovered too much.

"Fine... go look for her. Our house isn't that big, you know?" Reggie smiled and took the salad out of the fridge.

She searched the downstairs bathroom just off the kitchen and then the sunporch. No Paige. Just all three cats lounging on the sofa. Kate walked back through the kitchen and into the dining room. Everyone was seated around the table. The guys had all helped themselves to a drink and were munching on salad and Kate's homemade bread.

"No Paige?" Arlo asked.

Kate shook her head.

"Maybe she's in the basement."

"Dad, why in the world would she be down there?"

Arlo coughed and waved a hand in the air. "I dunno. But I found her down there the other day looking through old photos. She was curious about the ones with your mother."

"Oh?" Kate replied, tilting her head.

"Do you want me to go see if she's –"

Kate interrupted, "No, no. You guys eat up. I'll go."

Arlo got up from the table. "Kate, let me go. You and Reggie take care of dinner."

Their eyes locked for a moment, and then Kate turned away. "Okay, thanks Dad."

"You're welcome." Arlo walked past Kate and toward the basement door in the kitchen.

"Make sure you turn the light on at the top of the stairs," she warned.

"It's already on. Paige has to be downstairs."

"And hold on to the railing, Papa!"

"Fuck off, Victor!" Arlo shouted back, and everyone laughed.

CHAPTER 13
ARLO

September 27, 2019 – Friday

I found Paige in the basement sitting cross legged on a shag rug with her back up against the washing machine. She looked so tiny, with her boney knees poking through her leggings.

"Whatcha doing, kiddo?"

Paige had a cardboard box next to her on the floor, a few stacks of photographs were piled near her on the rug. "*Mom / Keep*" was written in black marker on one of the flaps of the box.

"Paige?" I asked because she hadn't yet looked up or answered me. In fact, she hadn't acknowledged my presence at all.

"Pappy?" she finally said after a few seconds.

"Yeah?" I knelt down next to her but wasn't sure if I could get back up if I chose to sit down beside her. Not with one good arm, anyway.

She held out a picture for me to look at. "Is this my mommy?"

I took the photo from her and examined it. It was an old picture, ripped at one corner. It was of me and Celeste, Sean and Kate. The kids were young there, younger than Parker and Paige were now. We were on a boardwalk, all four of us happy and tan. I flipped the picture over; sadly there was no date written on the back.

I held the picture in my right hand. "Mmm-hmm. This is your mom and Uncle Sean," I replied, pointing at it with my left hand. "And me and your Grandma Celeste... you remember me telling you about her?" Paige nodded. "We were at the beach. Bethany, I think."

"You're almost as tan as me here!"

I laughed, "You are correct, smart girl! Now c'mon. Let's take this box upstairs so everyone can have a look. What do you say? It's time for dinner. Your mom will be mad if we don't go up."

I stood up because my knees were killing me. "Ready, Paige?" I asked, turning toward the stairs.

Paige collected all of the pictures and put them back in the box. "Okay," she said reluctantly.

"That's a good girl. Let's go."

"Hey, Pappy?"

"Yeah?"

"Why did you say, 'fuck off' to Uncle Victor?"

I turned around quickly then hesitated for a second. *Oh, boy.* "Okay, listen Paige. That wasn't a nice thing to say. Don't say that word and don't tell your mom you heard me say it, okay?"

"Off?"

I almost laughed. *Kids.* "No, the other one."

Paige gave me a frown but nodded her head.

"Promise? I don't want to get in trouble with your mother. She can be ruthless."

"I promise, Pappy."

After dinner, we took turns looking through the box of old photos while Kate and Reggie cleaned up. Paige asked if she could take a few pictures and put them in her room, including the one of us at the beach she had shown me earlier. Reggie said yes, but I could tell Kate wanted to object, for whatever reason.

"Well, come on, kids. Let's get your teeth brushed and your pajamas on," Reggie instructed. "You can watch a movie in Parker's room if you want."

"Yay!" Paige said, but Parker just rolled his eyes. I don't think he was interested in having his little sister as a sleepover buddy.

Once the kids gave us all hugs and went upstairs, Kate found a deck of cards, and we started a game of euchre. Reggie wasn't much of a card player and said he had a few work emails to respond to. He stayed in the room with us but was lost in his own little world at the end of the table for a while. I could tell Kate was not happy about this, but she didn't say anything.

After several rounds, Victor announced he wanted to make his Moscow Mules. "Wanna help me, Sean?"

Sean, who already had a few of my beers, stood up, unsteady on his feet. "Sure thing, babe."

Kate laughed, while she dealt out another hand. "A little tipsy, brother? I think you two might want to consider staying over. It's a long drive back."

"I packed us both a bag," Victor chuckled. "I planned on getting soused. You with me, Reggie?"

"Man, Victor. You know I can't drink like the rest of you. I'm sure Arlo will take you up on it."

"I'm too old for that nonsense," I joked.

Kate got out a few bowls of snacks and set them in the middle of the table.

"Oh, Kate. We're all too full!" Reggie groaned playfully.

"Speak for yourself," Victor said, snatching a pretzel from the bowl with one hand and rubbing his belly with the other. He then took Sean by the arm, and the two of them retreated to the kitchen.

I took a quick look at my cards. "This hand looks more like a foot. Reggie, take over for me, will you?"

Without giving Reggie time to respond, I stood up and walked out of the room. I took the reprieve to walk over to my temporary home and grab a cigar. Once I got back to the bottom of the garage steps, I lit my Montecristo and strolled to the edge of the driveway. I was missing my wife, and being around the rest of my family made it worse.

After about fifteen minutes or so, I headed back inside, freezing and wishing I could easily rub my arms. *Damn cast.*

I stopped in the kitchen to wash my hands because I knew my daughter would scold me otherwise. I already got shit for smoking. After I shut off the water, I could hear the four of them whispering in the other room. They apparently hadn't heard me come back inside.

"Don't be so hard on her, Kate," I heard Sean say. "Oh, c'mon now, big brother. You don't actually think things are going to work out, *do you*? Natasha is obviously having an affair. Poor Dad."

I heard Reggie cough. "Kate, shhh."

"Listen, Dad loves Natasha. And we don't know what's really going on," Sean stated. "They've been married for ten years, Kate. It's time to give it up. You should want what's best for Dad."

Good boy, Sean, I thought. I wanted to hear more – yet *didn't* want to hear more – about what my kids had to say about my love life. So I stood in the middle of the kitchen, frozen in place. I felt like a little kid, caught doing something wrong, but not really.

"What about you, Victor?" Kate asked. "You're being unusually quiet."

"No comment," Victor retorted.

"I find that hard to believe!" Reggie joked, and they all laughed, except Victor.

"Honestly, Kate, I just don't want to talk about it."

"Talk about what? What *aren't* you saying, Victor?"

Victor cleared his throat but didn't say anything.

I wised up and opened the refrigerator door, hoping that if anyone came in, I would look preoccupied and not like I'd been eavesdropping for several minutes.

"*Victor*...?" Kate pressed.

"Victor had lunch with Natasha this week," Sean said, the words spilling from his lips. I could envision him slapping his hand over his mouth.

"What the hell, Sean?!" Victor scolded. He was no longer whispering.

"Oh, man," I heard Reggie say. Then I heard a chair scraping along the hardwood floor, and I hid my face in the fridge as if I was searching for something.

"Oh, hey, Arlo," Reggie said loudly, so the others knew I was back in the house. "Whatcha looking for?"

"Reggie, my man... I umm. I was gonna make a cup of coffee, but I wanted to make sure you had creamer first."

"I'm sorry, Arlo. I don't think we do. Here, let me check."

I moved aside so Reggie could look in the fridge. "You know what? It's fine. I'll just have another beer."

"You got it, boss." Reggie handed me a bottle. "You want to get another round of cards going?"

"Thanks. And yeah, sure. For a little while, anyway," I replied, trying to hide my anger. "One more drink and then I think I'm just about ready to call it a night."

CHAPTER 14
NATASHA

September 28, 2019 – Saturday

On Saturday afternoon, Joyce's younger sister, Bonnie, and her niece, Hazel, came to visit. They lived about an hour away in New York and would sometimes visit on the weekends. Bonnie's husband Ben was, according to Joyce, having an affair with a coworker. Bonnie knew about Ben's affair, but Joyce and I both agreed she probably wouldn't leave him. Bonnie didn't work, and it was apparent she didn't care to. And the woman really didn't have any marketable skills. Not to mention Ben raked in close to a half a million dollars annually. Even I could see why Bonnie stayed. Well, kind of. At least I understood.

Ben was always taking "work trips" that sometimes spilled over into the weekends. Joyce, whose own husband left her for a younger coworker, knew all too well the signs of an affair. I tried to mind my own business, especially when my own (third) marriage wasn't, to put it gently, in the best of places. So, after a quick lunch and forced small talk, I offered to watch Hazel while the sisters chatted in the kitchen.

Hazel was a sweet, tiny child. She had these big green eyes and dark red ringlets that I very much admired. She brought coloring books with her, so I suggested we go into the spare bedroom where I was staying and color pictures. There was more room on the floor in there. No matter how much I tried to tidy up Joyce's apartment, somehow all of the common spaces ended up a disaster again within half a day. Luckily, Joyce had left my temporary bedroom alone.

Hazel had a small backpack with her; it was pink and gray with cute little sayings on it like, "Cool!" and "You can do it!" She pulled out a few coloring books and displayed them proudly on the carpet. Then Hazel grabbed a soft pencil case from her backpack. It was stuffed full of crayons, colored pencils, and markers. Opening the zipper, Hazel dumped the contents on the floor. She looked up at me smugly. Apparently, I was supposed to be in awe of her stash.

I pulled two pillows off of the bed so we could lay down on our bellies.

"You've got quite the collection there, Hazel."

Hazel smiled proudly. "Thanks," she answered, flipping through a book with princesses. "I'm going to color this one," Hazel added, pointing to a Disney princess with long, wild hair like hers.

I thought of Paige and tried to remember which one was her favorite princess. *Mulan? Jasmine?* I guessed to myself. One time, on a rare occasion when Arlo and I were babysitting, Paige told me that I looked like Jasmine, with my long, dark hair. Only I had a bigger nose, she'd said. Paige tried telling me I looked "exotic" but called me "extinct" instead. I remember how Arlo and I laughed for days over it. Sweet Paige and her lack of a filter.

Hazel pointed at a book. "Do you want to color in this one." It wasn't really a question, rather a strong suggestion.

"Sure thing." I took the book and began flipping through the pages. This coloring book was full of baby animals. I selected one with little piggies and got to work.

"I heard you just had a birthday."

She nodded. "Mmm-hmm." I looked over at the girl, whose tongue was protruding ever so slightly from her lips as she concentrated on her artwork.

I heard Bonnie let out a small screech from the other room, and I could tell she was crying. Hazel's eyes flashed toward the doorway momentarily, but she was soon back to coloring.

"So how old are you now... twelve, thirteen?"

Hazel let out a little snort. "Ha! Noooo, Miss Natasha!"

"Twenty-seven?"

"I'm *five*!"

"Ohhh! Okay. Five, gotcha," I said, tapping her playfully on the arm with my pink crayon.

"How old are you?"

"Forty years older than you," I said.

"What?! That's old!" Hazel started to giggle.

I started to laugh too and tapped her again with the crayon. "Hey now, that's not nice." *If Hazel thinks I'm old, she would probably think Arlo is ancient!*

After I finished coloring the pigs, I searched through the colors and markers on the floor. "Where's all of the green ones?"

"I dunno. I go through them a lot because of coloring grass and trees and stuff."

"I see..." I responded, skimming through the pile. "Hazel, love... there's nothing here but a bunch of pieces. There's one green marker but it's dried up. And all of the green crayons are broken."

I was teasing her, naturally, but I was also mildly annoyed. I hadn't felt well all morning, and I hadn't had much to eat. It was starting to get to me.

"So?" she replied softly without looking up, that little bit of tongue still poking out.

All of a sudden, the side of my head started to pound.

"So? Well, girl, I think you need to step up your coloring game," I joked, rubbing my temple. "What am I supposed to do now?"

Hazel stopped coloring and looked up at me. "So? Color, Miss Natasha. Just because they're broken doesn't mean they don't work."

Touché.

I tilted my head back and forth a bit and frowned. "Hmm. Yeah, I guess you've got that right." I picked up a small bit of green crayon and started coloring in the grass. It was half the size of a regular crayon, and it was hard to hold. But still, it worked.

"See, your grass is still green," Hazel said, pointing at my picture with the tip of her crayon and scrunching her nose. "Adults are always so *worried* about things being broken."

I nodded. "Yeah, we are."

I held back the tears that started to form, though, because somehow this little girl, not even in kindergarten yet, just said something unbelievably profound and didn't even realize it. Somehow it struck me, this idea of me being broken but not dead. Broken but still with a lot of life left. Broken but still married to a man who loved me.

And yet, maybe not even broken at all. Just a smaller version of the person I once was, just like the little green crayon.

CHAPTER 15
ARLO

September 28, 2019 – Saturday

Shortly after we started playing cards again, I feigned a massive headache and retreated to my temporary home above the garage. I was so furious with the kids that I could barely stand to look at them. Kate, for assuming my wife was having an affair. Victor, for having lunch with Natasha and not telling me about it. Sean, for knowing about it and keeping it a secret from his old man. And Reggie, well... I shouldn't be mad at Reggie, but I was anyhow. Simply for being at the wrong place at the wrong time.

So, when my son and son-in-law came up to say goodbye, I said my pleasantries and tried to be cordial. But Sean and Victor could tell something was off.

"Still not feeling well, Papa?" Victor asked, taking a seat on the chair next to the couch where I was seated.

"I'm fine," I uttered. "Just sick of this cast, is all. I need to find my cigars." I spun around to see if I'd left them on the kitchen counter.

"You're not fine, dad," Sean retorted, taking a seat next to me on the couch. I looked down at Sean's legs. They were long and lean and, just like mine, his knees were almost touching the coffee table in front of us.

I scratched at an itch under my cast and just out of my reach. "I said I'm fine, son."

"Papa, come on now," Victor nudged, giving me a toothy grin.

I shot Victor a quick glance, but I didn't respond, just continued to scratch.

"Okay, well dad, we're off. Unless you need anything that is," Sean stated, rubbing his hands together, a sure sign he was getting antsy.

"You hung over?" I asked.

"Oh, yeah. Big time."

"Serves you right, drinking the way you did," Victor teased, slapping me on the leg and winking.

"Hey now, mister," Sean retorted. "It's not my fault I'm built the way I am. I can't drink as –"

"Ah! Are you calling me fat?!" Victor snorted, putting his hands up to his chest.

"Oh, please, Victor. I never said that... don't go twisting my words!"

So there I was, caught in between Sean and Victor in what appeared to be a regular argument for the two of them.

"Well, sorry I'm such a fat ass, Sean. Maybe you need to put on a few pounds, so you don't get trashed everywhere we go!"

"Come on, Victor! I –"

I couldn't take it any longer. "For fuck's sake, that's enough you two!" I yelled, standing up. "My God, you're acting like two teenage girls instead of grown men." I pointed at them both with my good hand. "And, if you want to know what's bothering me... well, I'd love to know why you had lunch with my wife, Victor, and failed to mention it to me."

I walked past Victor and into the kitchen, where I found a Montecristo on the kitchen counter and dropped it into my shirt pocket. I grabbed my mug and started to pour myself another cup of coffee.

"I told you, Victor... you should have told Dad," Sean scolded.

"Oh, you're no better, son," I snapped, turning toward Sean. "You kept it from me."

Sean rubbed his face with the palms of his hands. "I'm sorry, Dad. I felt like it was Victor's place to tell you," he said, turning and locking eyes with Victor, "not mine."

"Yet you had no problem telling Kate and Reggie, yeah?" I was acting like a teenage girl myself at the moment.

Victor nodded then exhaled slowly. "So, you overheard us talking last night?"

I didn't answer. I just shrugged my shoulders. I would have crossed my arms if I could. "I'm going out for a smoke."

With that, I turned and walked out the door, not even stopping to put my shoes on. Which was a stupid, stupid mistake, but I didn't dare go back inside. My socks quickly became wet from the cold, damp steps, and I looked and felt ridiculous. But there was no turning back now.

I stood at the end of the driveway, sans shoes, and puffed on my cigar. After roughly five minutes, I heard someone pad down the garage steps. It was Victor – I could tell from his footsteps – and he came to stand right next to me. I did everything I could to avoid looking at him. After a few moments, Victor cleared his throat, and I finally glanced over.

He was holding my boots up in the air by the laces.

I let out a long sigh then chuckled. "Thanks, Vic."

Victor tilted his head and kind of swung the boots a little. "Well?"

"Yes, thank you."

Victor bent down and held the right boot steady on the ground so I could slip my foot into it. I struggled since I had nothing to hold on to and because I was still puffing on my Montecristo, but I eventually got my feet in both boots with Victor's help.

It was humbling.

Damn. And now my boots were all wet from the socks. But I didn't have it in me to tell Victor.

Victor stood up and I patted him on the back. "I appreciate it."

He nodded, rubbing his hands together. "Papa, I'm sorry I didn't tell you about having lunch with Natasha. I know it seems like I'm being deceitful, but I promised her I wouldn't tell you. And, well, if I would have... that would have been dishonest, too. To her. Ya know?" Victor folded his arms and tilted his head to the side. I could see tears forming in the corners of his eyes. "I felt stuck in the middle."

I nodded. "Yeah, yeah. I get it. I'm sorry." I paused to step into the grass to put my cigar out on the ground, then added, "I just wish I knew what was going on with her."

Victor thought about this for a moment then replied, "Well, I can tell you this. There is good news and there is bad news."

"The good news?" I asked, again attempting to scratch that itch right under my cast.

"The reason she left... it's probably not what you're thinking."

"Okay. And the bad news?"

We both turned when we heard the apartment door open and saw Sean walk out. He stopped on the landing and peered down at us.

"The bad news?" I inquired once more.

Victor still had tears in the corners of both eyes that hadn't yet made their way down to his cheeks. "The bad news is... it's probably not what you're thinking."

CHAPTER 16
CORA

September 28, 2019 – Saturday

Two nights ago, Cora just *had* to go out to the garage and start digging around. It took her over an hour to go through Charlie's things, and she got two papercuts in the process. *Darn boxes!* And, really, all the flipping things that man had!

Charlie and Cora had been really quite different in that way. Cora despised clutter. But Charlie... well, he'd been a collector. He enjoyed acquiring stamps and rare coins and train sets. He got such a thrill out of finding new trinkets for his collections. She loved Charlie so, even though she hadn't loved all of the stuff, Cora hadn't said much about his hobbies. Even if his hobbies had cluttered up their beautiful house.

And even though Charlie had enjoyed his hoard of collectables, what he really had loved was bird watching. Before he'd gotten sick, Charlie would spend hours hiking. Reluctantly, sometimes Cora would go along. He had dozens of books on birds; Charlie had even kept a journal, where he'd logged what types of birds he'd seen, with the date and time. Preposterous, if you asked Cora. But she would just smile and roll her eyes, because it was what her husband loved to do, and she had loved him. Quirks and all.

So Cora knew that was where she would find Charlie's fancy binoculars, with all of the other belongings in the garage that she couldn't quite bear to part with. Charlie had had another, less expensive pair of binoculars, but Cora's youngest granddaughter broke those somehow.

And Cora needed them so she could keep an eye on her neighbors, especially the Beckford house.

The Beckfords! What were the odds that Cora would finally meet a nice, handsome man about her age and he was Kate's father! Were there no single men in Row Point Lake?

And it just so happened to be Kate Beckford's father.

Cora saw Kate and Reggie Beckford as troublemakers. Well, not so much them but those vulgar cats they had. That one was always coming into her yard – her garden! Peeing all over the place. It made her sick and, frankly, Cora couldn't say that she was sad that the one cat died. In fact, she wouldn't mind if all the other cats croaked, too. Coming into her yard and tearing up her garden, howling at night when Kate and Reggie forgot to let them inside. Honestly, this was supposed to be a *quiet* neighborhood...

Not to mention the kids! Paige and Parker (especially Parker!) were always playing out back and making such a ruckus. Not like Cora's three precious grandchildren who could sit and color or read or play on their tablets without any fuss or roughhousing or anything valuable getting broken. (Well, the binoculars... but that was a one-time occurrence.)

Another time, Parker had a friend over, and they were tossing a football back and forth. It sailed over Cora's fence and crushed her Carnival Azaleas. She could have screamed!

And well, Cora actually did scream. Inside her house, with her face pressed into Charlie's pillow. She was just so thankful her precious hydrangeas and butterfly bushes weren't damaged, too.

When Cora and Charlie first moved in, way before the Beckfords lived in Row Point Lake, she'd insisted they put up a fence for those very reasons. Reasons like footballs and water gun battles and roaming pets and cat urine. Charlie had wanted to get a chain link fence because it was inexpensive.

"But, Charlie, it will look cheap!" Cora had cried at the time.

Charlie and she had bickered for two weeks over a fence (a fence!). Cora had wanted a privacy fence, for when they had children and grandchildren of their own and, naturally, for Cora's garden. Charlie said it looked off-putting. Cora had retorted that the chain link was off-putting.

In the end, they'd agreed upon a wooden picket fence, and it was rather quite lovely. But it did not keep cats or kids or footballs out of the yard...

What happened to that little Beckford girl getting so sick like that... well, Cora wouldn't wish that on any parent, not even the Beckfords. Cora didn't think anyone knew what really happened. The police came around at the time, asking if Cora had any information. Ha! Incompetent *idiots*. They never solved squat. Don't get her started on those police officers. They couldn't catch a cold, let alone a criminal.

Cora had been dealing with Charlie's cancer then, and he'd been very sick. Close to the end, she knew. So, whatever had happened to Paige Beckford, Cora couldn't have said. And she'd told the police that very thing.

Not much happened in Row Point Lake. Funny thing though, that the police hadn't taken a closer look at the parents. With Kate being a nurse and Reggie an occupational therapist – both in the medical field, so to speak – you'd think that the pair would have seen the signs that their daughter was sick.

It seemed Cora would have to keep a close eye on the Beckford home.. Closer than before, at least. And how had she never met Arlo before? He seemed like a pretty active grandparent, involved in the kids' lives quite a bit.

She did remember seeing an older gentleman over at the house now and again, but Cora never got a good look at him. Not until the other day, that is. And she recalled a younger, fairly attractive (albeit exotic) woman at the Beckford's on occasion. And both of them were there quite often, just around the time the cat had died, and the girl had gotten sick, Cora remembered now. She would sit on the back porch when Charlie had napped (which was quite often near the end) and drink her tea. And she did remember seeing the two of them – Arlo and Natasha – in and out of the house for a few weeks.

Cora had assumed Natasha was Kate's friend or sister. But after her conversation with Arlo... oh! To know she is Kate's stepmother! That surely came as a shock. The disdain

Kate Beckford must have felt, knowing that her stepmother was not much older than her. Well, Cora had to admit that it did make her smile a little.

CHAPTER 17
KATE

September 29, 2019 – Sunday

At least once a month, Kate's family attended church with her in-laws, who lived about an hour away. Afterwards, Reggie's mom would prepare lunch, and they'd spend the afternoon talking and playing board games or putting puzzles together. Kate asked her dad if he wanted to join them, but he'd declined.

Needless to say, Arlo was still pissed at her.

Kate had seen her dad just briefly the day before, outside when he was talking to Sean and Victor. *Of course, he'd talk to them. But her, no.* He'd be upset with Kate for days. His only daughter, and the one he came to stay with after he broke his arm and had a concussion.

The only one to give him grandchildren.

Reggie said to let her dad be, give him some time to cool off. Reggie was always all about cooling off. Kate didn't know how he could be so calm about everything all of the damn time. *Only sociopaths have such a lack of emotion, right?*

But Reggie was no sociopath. And he was no idiot. So, Kate did as her husband said and left her dad alone. For the time being, at least.

When they got back from visiting, Reggie didn't park in the garage; he didn't want to disturb Arlo.

Arlo never came out to say hello to her or the kids. So later in the evening, after Parker and Paige showered and settled in for the night, Kate crossed the driveway and headed up the outside garage stairs. She knocked lightly on one of the small glass panes of the door. She tried to peer inside, but couldn't because of the curtain. It was semi-opaque, but Kate could still see movement in the living room.

Her hand went up to the doorknob, but she stopped herself. Even though this was her house, her garage, Kate didn't dare invade her father's privacy by testing the doorknob, as badly as she wanted to.

Instead, she called out softly, "Dad? Can I come in?"

She could still see a figure moving about.

Kate gently tapped on the window again. "Dad?"

He came to the door and opened it but just enough to peer out. "I'm on the phone," he answered.

"Can we talk? Please?"

"Just a minute, Kate. I'm on the phone," he said then shut the door.

Well, this is a new side of Arlo Callan. Or at least the one she hadn't seen in a long, long time.

So Kate stood on the landing of her own steps, *like a damn moron,* for what seemed like twenty minutes. But it was more like four minutes; she tapped her foot, counting the seconds as she waited. There had been two hundred and thirty seven taps before Arlo opened the door and gestured for her to come in.

"Can I sit?"

"It's your place." His tone was cold, distant.

Now, this was the Arlo that Kate recalled from years earlier. The one from right after her had mom died. The one who couldn't articulate his feelings, who was bitter and moody. Who wouldn't seek counseling or talk to his family doctor. The father that poured all of his time and attention into taking care of Sean and her and building that goddamn, ridiculous garbage empire. All so he didn't have to admit how sad he was.

This was the Arlo that she knew before he had grandchildren to love. And even though Kate loathed the idea of admitting it, that was also her dad before he met Natasha.

After he met and quickly *fell in love* with Natasha, her dad became a new man. Wait, not necessarily *new*. A changed man, maybe. A better man.

Well, damn.

Kate took a seat on the sofa. "How's your arm?" She gestured in his general direction.

Arlo sat down in one of the chairs, propping his right arm up on the armrest. "I mean, it's been better."

Kate parted her lips to speak, but then couldn't think of the right words to say, so she stopped herself.

"I'm going home after my doctor's appointment on Wednesday. Hopefully, I'll get out of this cast. But even if not, I need to go back home."

"Okay," she replied and nodded.

Kate frowned slightly and bit her lip; she could feel the tears starting to form. "Dad... I'm really sorry about everything. About what I said..."

He stood up and walked to the fridge, pulled out a bottle of beer, not offering Kate one. "You never cared for Natasha. I get that. But there's no need to be cruel, Kate."

"I know..."

"*You don't actually think things are going to work out, do you? Natasha is obviously having an affair*," he muttered, sitting back down. Quoting her words, the words he overheard when eavesdropping. Using them against her.

Arlo set the beer down on the coffee table in front of them, and Kate silently cringed when he didn't use a coaster. She slid her hands under her thighs to stop herself from grabbing one from the end table and shoving it under the bottle.

"I mean, damn, Kate." Arlo sat back in the chair and threw his hands up.

"Dad, listen... I was out of line. I know that. But what did you expect? Natasha is closer to my age than yours. She's beautiful. And I'm not saying you're not a catch, but she's been married and divorced twice before. No kids. What makes you think she was going to be in it for the long haul?"

Shit. Kate actually said too much of what she was thinking. As usual.

"You have no idea what you're talking about. Natasha and I are in love. She's my wife, for heaven's sake. We've been married for a decade," he said, leaning forward in his chair and taking a sip from his beer bottle.

He's acting like a teenage boy, a puppy dog, Kate thought

angrily. "Then why'd she leave?" Kate questioned, shaking her head, her eyes wide. "Answer me that, Dad. If you two are so *in love*, why'd she leave?"

"I don't know," he replied, "I really don't know."

CHAPTER 18
REGGIE

September 30, 2019 – Monday

Most mornings, Reggie left the house before Kate and the kids. Thank goodness. There was so much arguing between Kate and Paige; some days he just couldn't take it. And that morning was no exception – Reggie couldn't take the endless bickering and left as soon as he could get his ass in gear.

Since Paige was only six years old, Kate and Reggie explained away many of her issues as being long-term effects from the illness. Which, naturally, was truthful *and* a huge part of it. "Cognitive delays" was the term the doctors used. But what that in fact looked like was a young girl with trouble sleeping, persistent and severe headaches, the inability to focus, communication delays, difficulty running and sometimes even walking fast, and wetting the bed at times.

And Reggie was at a loss. Here he was, an *occupational therapist* and couldn't even help his own daughter. Not that he got much, if any, support from Kate who continued to ignore it all.

Health care professionals, his ass.

Reggie walked through the kitchen and filled up the cats' water and food bowls along the way. He wasn't even to the doorway when Gwynn, the Calico, came from out of nowhere and immediately started attacking the food dish, while he cried loudly. Reggie left through the side door and spied the fat, gray cat Banks lounging on the floor. He was perfectly positioned so a beam of sunlight ran across his big belly. The chubby thing looked utterly content and kind of like a furry beached whale.

"Hey, Mr. Sunshine," Reggie said, laughing to himself and leaning down to rub Banks' belly for a moment. Of all the pets, Banks was his favorite, although Reggie loved them all. They were the family cats, but really, Reggie was the one who took care of them. "Where's your brother, huh?" he questioned, like Banks was actually going to tell him.

Reggie stood up and reached for his laptop bag when he spotted something out of the corner of his eye outside, through the back window. It was Baylor, skinny and tan – Reggie was sure it was him. Baylor was lying on his side in the grass with a leaf across his tail. And Reggie knew he was dead.

Oh, no. Poor Baylor. No... not today. Not now.

He walked outside and around the back of the house. Reggie bent down and touched Baylor's head. It was cold. *Oh, no.* Scooping Baylor up and holding him close, all Reggie could think was that he didn't want the kids or Kate to see him. Not right before school; they'd obviously be upset.

Not devastated, not like Reggie. But still, the kids would be upset.

Without giving it much thought, Reggie cradled the poor cat in his arms like a baby. Baylor was cold and his fur was stiff from the morning chill that lingered.

But Baylor couldn't have been out there that long, Reggie thought. He'd fed the cats just before bed last night and he was sure that Baylor had been there, begging with the other two. Of that Reggie was certain.

Reggie ascended the garage stairs and tapped lightly on the door. Arlo appeared after a few moments, and opening the door, he looked at Reggie and then at Baylor. Without saying a word, he ushered Reggie in.

"Well, shit," Arlo said, rubbing a hand through his hair. "What the hell happened here?"

"Man, I don't know Arlo. I was leaving for work and there he was… in the yard out back." He crossed the living room and pulled a bath towel from the narrow linen closet next to the bathroom. Carefully, Reggie laid it out as best he could on the carpet near the couch. He set Baylor down on the towel and wrapped him up in it.

"What are you going to do?" Arlo asked, taking a seat on the chair.

Reggie stood up and shook his head. "Can I leave him here until after work? I don't know what else to do. I don't want Kate to have to handle this," he said, making a rather senseless gesture toward the cat. "Kate's been really… anxious lately, not sure if you've noticed…"

Arlo nodded and shrugged. "Mmm. Well, should we call the police?"

Reggie shook his head and squinted. "What? Why?" His

father-in-law could be so dramatic at times; Reggie figured that was where Kate got it from.

Arlo leaned forward and rested his elbows on his knees. "Well, what if the cat was poisoned, like the other one?"

He guffawed. "Oh, you're serious? Really, Arlo?"

"Yeah, I am Reggie."

"C'mon now. You don't think that someone really poisoned Gibson and then, what... three years later poisoned another one of our cats, do you?" He looked down at the pitiful feline and hesitated for a second. "I mean, that was... my cousin Andrea said Gibson could have had a number of different problems..."

"I don't think so." Arlo said, getting up and walking into the kitchen. "But what do I know? Coffee?"

"No, thanks. Listen, I have to run. Please don't say anything to Kate. I have a break today. I'll swing by and take care of the cat." Remembering he left his laptop bag in the house, Reggie added, "I really have to go. I'm sorry to put you in this spot."

Arlo began pouring himself a cup of coffee but then stopped and looked at Reggie. "I'll handle the cat. Don't worry about stopping on your break."

"Are you sure?"

"Positive. I'll figure something out."

CHAPTER 19
ARLO

September 30, 2019 – Monday

I'll figure something out. *Well shit.*
That's what I said to Reggie, "I'll figure something out." *Like an idiot.*

I sat at the kitchen counter. I sipped my coffee slowly because I wasn't sure what to do next. So I stalled.

Should I call the cops? I shouldn't. Reggie would be upset with me. Kate never believed that Gibson was poisoned on purpose and, although Reggie initially had his doubts, he did eventually side with Kate that it must have been accidental. Or something else altogether that killed that cat. Not to mention that Paige had been everyone's top priority at the time. And not to mention that no one believed that my granddaughter – just a toddler at the time – had been poisoned on purpose. I mean, who would want to hurt Paige?

Once Paige began to recover, it really didn't matter what happened. We were all just so grateful that Paige survived. So, Kate and Reggie decided to forget about the why and how and be grateful that Paige was, at least somewhat, back to her old self. We all moved on. In fact, Natasha and I were the only ones who still had our doubts.

Natasha. Yes, of course. It was funny how after such a short time without my wife being by my side, I quickly forgot how much I relied on her for, well, almost everything. Advice, a shoulder to cry on, support.

I called her phone, but it went straight to voicemail. Instead of leaving a message, I hung up and maneuvered my cell phone to use the voice recorder thing that Sean showed me and sent Natasha a text message. It was lengthy and basically unreadable. Hell, half the words were not even close to being right. But I sent it anyway.

Exasperated, I stood up and walked over to the chair in the living area. I stared at Baylor, still wrapped up in the towel. Okay, well yes, that part was obvious, the cat was dead. But a small part of me felt like I just saw him move. No, he couldn't have moved. I touched Baylor, and he was as stiff as a board.

I picked up my phone and called Joyce, who answered on the second ring.

"Hi, Arlo."

"Oh, hey there, Joyce. I'm sorry to bother you so early..."

"Not a problem. I just left the house for work. What's up?"

"I'm trying to get a hold of Natasha. Her phone's going straight to voicemail, and, you see, it's kind of urgent I speak with her."

"Shoot, I'm sorry. She had a doctor's appointment this

morning. She's probably there by now, and that's why she's not answering."

Joyce didn't ask me what was so urgent, and I appreciated her for that. I always liked Joyce. Not only was she one of my wife's best friends but she was honest and hardworking. The kind of person that demanded respect. And, despite me being much older than Natasha, Joyce always thought we made a great couple. Another reason I liked her.

"Is Natasha all right?" I asked. "I didn't know she had a doctor's appointment coming up."

Where in the hell was this doctor's appointment?

Joyce hesitated, and I could hear her sigh heavily. "I feel like that's a question you better ask Natasha. I'm sorry, Arlo, I don't want to speak for her."

"Oh." I took a moment to process what Joyce just said and rationalized that she was being thoughtful. And neutral. Again, yet another one of the many reasons I liked Joyce, so I couldn't be upset with her. "Thanks, Joyce. I'll try calling her back later."

"You're welcome, Arlo."

Now I had more questions than I did five minutes ago.

An hour later, I was sitting on the back deck – *my* back deck – and drinking a glass of iced tea with my buddy Harvey. We were both enjoying a Montecristo and not saying much at first.

About fifteen minutes after Reggie left, Kate and the kids had come out of the house. I'd put my boots on and stood at the top of the landing. Parker and Paige had both run up the steps. Parker had given me an awkward left-handed high-five and Paige a long, squishy hug. And I'd loved both just the same.

Kate had waved to me from the driveway, and I'd raised a hand in response. We still hadn't been on the best of terms. I'd watched as all three of them piled into Kate's car, and Kate backed out of the driveway.

After they'd left, I'd waited about five minutes and then scooped up Baylor in the towel and taken him out to my car. I'd decided that I would forget about the possibility that the poor feline could have been poisoned and I would convince myself it was simply old age that killed him... how old was this cat anyway?

Before I'd backed out of the driveway, I'd called my old pal Harvey, who was also retired and lived just a few houses down from me.

"Arlo, my man! How the hell are you? How's the arm?" he'd asked. Harvey was also perpetually in a good mood.

"I'm doing okay. I go back to the doctor's this Wednesday." I'd sighed heavily. "Listen, Harvey... are you busy? I sort of need a favor."

I'd known that Harvey would help me if he was available because we'd been friends for the better part of thirty years. And the man loved Natasha's cooking, and we'd had him over on many occasions for dinner, an invitation he always graciously accepted. Plus, Harvey lived alone and didn't do much except tinker out in his garden or garage, like me. So, yeah, I was sure he'd be available.

"Do you want a beer?" I asked, pulling myself from my reverie.

"Nah. This is good," Harvey said, raising his iced tea glass. The tea was freshly brewed. I went about making a pitcher before Harvey helped me with Baylor.

I cleared my throat, then sat up straight in my chair. "Thanks, Harvey. I couldn't have buried him by myself. Not like this." I nodded in the direction of my bum arm.

"Not a problem, Arlo," Harvey said, swatting a hand in the air. "Anyhow, I'm sure I owe you a favor for something or other," he laughed.

Harvey was in his early sixties and in great shape. He was on the shorter side, but he still had all of his hair and was perpetually tan. Being a lifelong bachelor with no kids suited Harvey; although, I knew he got lonely at times. He'd never said it, but I could tell. There were things you merely came to know and understand about a person after you've known them so long, even if they never came out and said it.

"Yeah, well you did break my mower last summer," I joked back.

"Didn't I buy you a new one?"

I paused and scratched my chin. *I really needed a shave.* "Ha! Come to think of it, you did! But regardless... I appreciate it." I took a few puffs of my cigar.

"You think the bobcat will get to him?"

"I dunno," I answered. "I guess it doesn't matter either way."

Harvey took a long sip from his glass and set it on the table. "True."

We sat for a minute or two in silence and then Harvey looked over at me and chuckled.

"What?" I asked.

"You know, Arlo," Harvey began, "You've really come full circle, haven't you?" His smile was as big as the Cheshire Cat's.

"And why's that?" I asked suspiciously.

Harvey stood up and made his way to the railing then turned to look at me. "So, you fell down the steps, *these* steps," he joked, pointing toward the stairs. "You go stay at Kate's house. One of their dozen or so cats died... and now you're back here, burying the cat. You know, I probably wouldn't be here helping you with the cat if you hadn't broken your arm."

I smiled back. "Circle of life, my friend."

"When's your wife coming home, anyway?"

I shrugged. "Your guess is as good as mine."

"I'm in need of a good meal. I miss her cooking." Harvey took a puff of his cigar.

"Me too, my man. Me too."

CHAPTER 20
KATE

September 30, 2019 – Monday

Parker and Paige headed to their classrooms, while Kate went to the nurse's office. It was the one part of Kate's day that she really enjoyed, seeing that her children got to their classes safely. Knowing that she was just down the hall.

Although Kate enjoyed her job as a school nurse, she had wanted to go on to become a nurse anesthetist. And Kate would have gotten there, making well over six figures, had she finished her master's degree.

And Kate could have done it. She was intelligent enough, and school came easily for Kate. No, that hadn't been the issue for her. Life simply became harder, busier. Kate and Reggie married and then Parker came along.

Kate struggled with postpartum depression. She couldn't concentrate on her studies, not even her online courses. Even simple tasks like feeding the baby became daunting. She found herself seeking escapes, yet ironically, too exhausted to execute any of her ideas.

Such was life.

As it was, Kate knew it was going to be a hell of a day. First, she and her dad were still not really in a great place. And that had really gotten to her. And, worse yet, Reggie was going to be so *miserable* all day because of Baylor. Kate cared about the cats too. But not like Reggie. They'd adopted all four cats (*now two*) before the kids were born, so they were getting up in age. Finding one dead cat wasn't the most surprising thing to happen.

But still.

Oh, Reggie. He'd be upset all day about Baylor. Not to mention the stress of knowing he was going to have to tell the kids and Kate about the cat. Naturally, Kate would act surprised. She wouldn't want him to know that she knew Baylor was dead because then Reggie would ask why she just left him outside there like that. Kate thought Reggie could be so sensitive. Soft.

But the real puzzle was, what did Reggie do with Baylor? Because his body hadn't been in the yard when Kate and the kids left the house.

Did Reggie put the cat in his car and take him to work with him? She thought that seemed unlikely. And there wouldn't have been time to bury him. Did Reggie get her dad involved? That idea was not probable, but possible. And, of course, Kate couldn't have asked her dad. Not after how they ended things yesterday. *Well*, Kate supposed, *I'll find out soon enough.*

She busied herself with paperwork for close to an hour, but she had other things on her mind, so it was hard to concentrate. It took everything Kate had to stay off her cell phone.

Kate was distracted because two kids came down from class to see her. The younger students always liked visiting the school nurse. They thought it was important, and they liked getting out of class, even if it was just for a few minutes.

Her first visitor was a little boy, a kindergartener, who had a small cut on his finger. Kate put a dab of Neosporin on it and a bandage and sent him back to his classroom with a note to take home to his parents.

The second kid was a third-grade girl who was in Parker's class. She came to see Kate often, usually twice a week.

"Hello, Nurse Beckford," she said, knocking lightly on Kate's door, which was half open.

"Hi, Josie," she answered, swinging her chair to face the girl. With her dark, wavy hair and big gray eyes, the young girl was a real beauty. But Josie always looked sad. *Understandably so,* Kate thought, *but still sad.*

Kate smiled. "What can I do for you, hon?"

"My arms are itchy again," she said, pouting. The pitiful thing had severe eczema, but it usually went untreated. Josie lived with her grandmother, who was sweet but forgetful and had plenty of her own health issues. Josie's dad was well... who the hell knew who he was.

Josie's mom Tara was in and out of the house. She was unreliable, couldn't hold a job, and cared more about men than her own daughter. Tara was supposedly a recovering addict, but Kate was pretty sure she was still using. And Kate happened to know that Tara was currently staying at the house with Josie, but Kate doubted it would be for long. It never was.

"Have a seat," Kate urged gently, and Josie sat down in the hard plastic chair across from Kate's desk.

Kate got a tube of ointment out and a pack of crackers she had in her desk drawer. She knew Josie liked the peanut butter ones the best. But Kate wasn't supposed to have them because of all of the allergies the students had. She thought about sneaking them in anyway, but if the secretary Ms. Simpson found out, she would ensure Kate was reprimanded. And how would that have looked, the school nurse causing some poor child to go into anaphylaxis.

Kate donned a pair of latex gloves and asked Josie to roll her sleeves up. She examined both of Josie's arms and was pleasantly surprised to see that her dry skin wasn't all that red, not as bad as usual. Just a few patches of dry skin. Although they were exceptionally red and dry, probably from all of her scratching.

"Are you itchy anywhere else?" Kate asked Josie, praying the answer was no.

Josie shook her head. Kate applied cream to both arms and waved her hands so the cream would dry.

"You can pull your sleeves down," she said to the girl.

After Kate took off her gloves and washed her hands, she gave Josie the crackers.

"Thank you, Nurse Beckford."

"You're welcome, hon. Do you want a drink?"

Josie nodded, so Kate grabbed her a juice box from her mini fridge and handed it to Josie too.

Kate sat across from Josie, and they chatted while Josie ate crackers and drank juice. Kate asked Josie about her home life, like she always did. And, over time, the girl told

Kate quite a bit because Josie trusted her. Kate was the school nurse, after all.

"How's your mom?"

Josie shrugged. "Mom's mom."

"Is she using again?" Kate knew she shouldn't ask her this, but she did anyway.

Josie took a few bites before answering. "I dunno," she replied, and a few crumbs spilled from her mouth. Kate pretended not to notice. "She's seeing someone, though. A man."

"Oh?" she said, feigning surprise.

Josie nodded and sipped her juice. "Yeah."

Kate crossed her legs, uncrossed them. She sat on her hands, so she didn't fidget too much. Not like Josie would have noticed. "What makes you think that?"

"My grandma said that she is gone a lot during the day. And I know she's not working," Josie remarked, nibbling on another cracker. Crumbs spilled. "I saw him drop her off a few times after I got home from school." She paused. "I wish I just had a normal mom, ya know?"

"Yes, I do."

Josie finished her snack and threw the garbage away. She crossed her legs on the chair and, nervously, wrapped her long curls around both index fingers, a tell-tale sign that Josie was now done with their conversation.

"Thank you for the cream. And the snack. I guess I better get back to Mrs. Orion's class."

Kate nodded, trying not to show her disappointment. "That's probably a good idea. I'll write you a note."

CHAPTER 21
NATASHA

September 30, 2019 – Monday

When I got out of my doctor's appointment, I saw a cryptic text from Arlo. Something about one of Kate and Reggie's cats. He was probably using the talk-to-text feature again, which he was terrible at. I also had a text message from Joyce that Arlo called her looking for me and he sounded "unnerved." Her term, not mine.

I'd been thinking about my coloring slash therapy session with five-year-old Hazel over the weekend. I'd been so selfish not to talk to Arlo about what was going on. We had been married for a decade, after all. My third husband, but the one I'd been with the longest. And the only man who truly loved me, and I truly loved in return.

Once I was back at Joyce's apartment, I pulled a can of ginger ale from the fridge then took a seat in the living room, before calling Arlo. He answered after a few rings.

"Oh! Natasha, I'm so glad you called me back. Joyce said you had an appointment, and I hated to bother you..."

I interrupted, "Arlo, is everything all right?"

"Well. I don't know. You see, something strange happened. Reggie found Baylor dead outside this morning..."

Arlo went on to tell me the whole story about Reggie wrapping the cat up in a blanket, Arlo promising to take care of Baylor, taking the cat to our house, and finally asking Harvey to help him bury the cat in the backyard.

He sighed. "That's the whole story. Harvey just left a few minutes ago. I didn't know what else to do."

I rubbed my eyes. "And what do you think, Arlo?"

"About the cat?"

My hand was beginning to go numb, so I switched the phone into my left hand. "Yes, the cat. What do you think happened to him?"

"I honestly can't say, Natasha. I mean, to assume the two incidents are related seems a little far-fetched, doesn't it? But, anything is possible, and I said as much to Reggie. Asked him his thoughts. But Reggie wanted no parts of my speculation."

"It's possible the cat just died from natural causes. I mean, they all have to be pretty old, right?" I asked, standing up. I headed to my temporary bedroom and took my bags out of the closet.

"Do you think it's possible that someone has a vendetta against Kate or Reggie? That they'd want to hurt them, so they hurt the cats?"

I opened up a drawer and started pulling out my socks, bras, and underwear. I tossed them on the bed. "That doesn't explain Paige. Unless, of course, that was intentional too. But I doubt that."

"Right, I agree," Arlo said.

"I hate to use the words 'collateral damage' when we're talking about your granddaughter, but maybe it was just an accident that she got injured when really someone was targeting cats. You know how messed up people are. Arlo?"

There was a long pause. "Sorry, what was that? I dropped the phone. Damn arm. I can't wait until I get this cast off. Anyway, I'm sorry. What were you saying?"

"Nothing. It's not important. Listen, are you home now?" I asked, shoving my sandals into a tote bag.

"Yeah."

"Will you stay there?"

"Sure, if you tell me why?"

"We need to talk in person," I answered. "I'm coming home."

CHAPTER 22
REGGIE

September 30, 2019 – Monday

A little after lunchtime, Reggie was in between clients and called Arlo from his car. Just when Reggie thought he was going to get Arlo's voicemail, he finally answered.

"Reggie, hi."

"Hi, Arlo. How did it go with Baylor?" he asked nervously. Reggie took a sip of his gas station coffee and frowned.

"Good. I took care of him."

His father-in-law didn't elaborate, so Reggie hesitated for a moment, wondering if he was done with his explanation.

"Okay, so... what did they say?"

"Who's *they*?"

Reggie frowned again and pulled over into the parking lot of a strip mall. "The vet, Arlo. Did you take Baylor to Andrea? What did she say?"

"I didn't take Baylor to Andrea or any other veterinarian. I buried him. On my property."

Reggie paused to take this unexpected information in when Arlo added, "Well, Harvey actually buried the cat. I obviously couldn't do it alone. Not with this cast."

At first, Reggie wondered if he should be worried or even angry. But he wasn't. Baylor was dead, and taking him to the vet was not going to bring him back. Parker and Paige liked the cats. Kate tolerated them. He was the one who was and would be the most upset about Baylor...

"We put him behind one of the sheds. The one furthest from the house. Reggie?"

"Yeah," he said, snapping out of his stream of consciousness. "Sorry, Arlo. I'm here."

"Are you mad? Shit! I guess I thought since he was already gone..."

"No, no. It's all good. Maybe we just don't say anything to Kate or the kids. At least not yet."

"Sure. Whatever you want, Reggie. What are you going to say?" he asked, and Reggie realized that he didn't have any idea.

"I don't know. Maybe we don't say anything. Just pretend he ran away?"

"Whatever you want, man. It's not like I put up a grave marker. Although I could if you wanted me to."

"No. Let's just forget it," Reggie stated.

"Okay. Oh! By the way, I won't be there for dinner."

"No?"

"No, I talked to Natasha, and she's coming home!" Reggie thought Arlo sounded more like a teenage boy on his first date than a grandfather talking about his wife.

Well, hell. This was good *and* bad news, Reggie thought. "Oh, that's great, Arlo. So you're not coming back to the house? What should I tell Kate?"

Kate. *Ugh.*

"Hmmm. I don't know if Natasha is staying or just coming home to talk. Either way, I'll swing by this evening or in the morning to get my things. But I'm ready to stay home. I just need a ride to my appointment on Wednesday and Natasha already agreed to take me, regardless. Just tell Kate whatever you think is best."

They hung up. Reggie rolled down the window. It was a chilly day, even with the sun directly overhead. Still, he needed fresh air. Kate was going to have a meltdown. She'd be furious to find out Natasha was coming back.

Kate had always been jealous of her, Reggie knew. She felt like Natasha took her dad from her, even though Kate was in her twenties when Arlo and Natasha started dating. And Reggie and Kate were together by then, playing house. Nonetheless, Reggie knew that in Kate's mind, Natasha was the devil and out to take her dad's money, even though the woman has plenty of her own resources.

Kate was always immature in that way, and Reggie chalked a lot of Kate's misgivings to losing her mother at a young age.

This was not the day to be running late, Reggie knew. In fact, it was probably a night to distract the family. Maybe they could all go to the playground after dinner...

Wait! Parker has basketball practice. *Yes, even better,* Reggie surmised. He could take Parker to practice and wouldn't have to be around Kate.

He needed to make another phone call, but chickened out and sent a text instead.

Can't come by tonight. Sorry. Something came up. So sorry. I'll make it up to you, promise. xoxo

CHAPTER 23
NATASHA

September 30, 2019 – Monday

It was a little over an hour's drive from Joyce's apartment to our house in the Poconos. Before leaving, I sent Joyce a quick text message to thank her for her unending kindness and hospitality and to let her know I was going home.

She wrote back within a minute. *About damn time! Call me tomorrow, love you.*

I laughed as I took one more quick glance around Joyce's apartment to make sure I hadn't forgotten anything. I couldn't help taking a few moments to tidy up, even though I knew Joyce would make a royal mess of things again in no time. I hated to think of how she lived when I wasn't around.

My stomach was still queasy, so I took two more cans of ginger ale and a bottle of water from the fridge before heading out.

The entire drive, I ruminated on what I was going to say

to Arlo. Was he going to forgive me for keeping this huge secret from him?

The truth was he'd probably forgive me, which made me feel even more guilty. I'd been so selfish. My husband, who was pushing seventy years old, fell and fractured his arm. And here I was avoiding him like the plague.

What an asshole I'd been.

My first husband told me that I was selfish, and I probably was. We'd been young and I had still wanted to have fun and go out with my friends. Our marriage hadn't last long.

I thought the second time around, with a man slightly older than myself and more worldly, would be better. Alas, that marriage failed miserable too. I had been well established by this point, invested well, and he couldn't control me.

Meeting Arlo had been a blessing. I loved our life and the quiet, peaceful existence we shared. Arlo was retired and looking for someone to love unconditionally. I was immediately attracted to him. Arlo was handsome – tall, with strong and rugged features. I could tell he had a kind soul. He reminded me of my father, which may or may not be something I'd discussed in therapy over the years.

Naturally, Arlo and I had some issues, the main one being Kate and her disdain for me. I understood children not caring for their stepmother or stepfather because they felt as if their dad or mom was replacing their biological parent. But Kate was already an adult when Arlo and I met, for crying out loud. I never thought she'd hate me the way she did. *Does.* Whether I had taken Celeste's place or put a proverbial wall in between her and her dad, well... it was inconsequential.

I learned over the years that Kate was not well. She was a highly intelligent woman and, truthfully, could have been a doctor. A surgeon, maybe, if she had pursued that path. But Kate was content as a school nurse, which of course there was nothing wrong with. But Kate used the position to oversee her children and be close to home, where she could keep tabs on her husband. Kate was the Big Brother of the Beckford household.

Kate was whip-smart, yes. But emotional intelligence was a whole other ballgame that Kate was not equipped to play. She was scattered yet methodical, which, I felt, was a concerning combination. Needless to say, I tried to give Kate a wide berth.

I was just outside of town, less than ten minutes from home, when I saw one of the local community parks just up ahead on my left. At the last minute, I decided to pull over and make a quick turn into the parking lot. The park was known for its walking and hiking trails and was very popular. Even in the early afternoon on a Monday, the lot was already half full. Or half empty, depending on how you looked at it, I supposed.

I backed into a space and rolled down my car window then killed the engine. There were a few young moms with strollers gathered in a circle at the corner of the lot. They were chatting and drinking from their tumblers. A few avid hikers, mostly younger and middle-aged people, were dressed in workout attire and hiking boots. An older couple, I assumed to be in their late sixties, were holding hands and walking to their car. They were obviously in love; you could see it in the way they looked at each other while they talked.

The woman leaned over and rubbed her husband's arm, and then they both laughed. Some sort of inside joke between the two of them that I knew nothing about. Yet I smiled and laughed, too.

CHAPTER 24
REGGIE

September 30, 2019 – Monday

Reggie was at his last client's house of the day. It was James, a middle-aged man who had suffered a pretty severe stroke. James was a professor at a local university and taught African American Studies for over twenty years. At their appointments, Reggie chatted with James about his grandfather and their shared love of baseball. James lightheartedly ragged on Reggie about the Pittsburgh Pirates, and Reggie let him.

He'd taken a liking to James, which was something that happened from time to time due to working personally with clients like Reggie did. James was divorced and had two daughters in their late twenties. They didn't live with him, but both women came by often, at least once every day since James had his stroke two months before.

Nia was the younger of the two sisters. She wasn't married but had a long-term boyfriend who she shared twin boys with. Reggie liked James, so he didn't dare tell him that he'd slept with Nia. They had sex in the bathroom once, when James fell asleep, and Reggie was supposed to be jotting down a daily schedule of exercises for him. They screwed in his car once. That one almost got Reggie caught because Nia's lip gloss had fallen out of her pocket, either by accident or on purpose. But either way, it had rolled under the seat, and Parker found it. Reggie said it must have been his mom's and apparently that was all an eight year-old boy needed for an explanation. *Thank God.*

After that, Reggie told Nia he thought it was best that they kept their distance from each other. She agreed, yet a week later she messaged him, and they met up at a hotel just outside of town.

Luckily for Reggie, Nia said she was going to be taking a new job, so she wouldn't be able to sneak away to see Reggie as often. It was better that way, Reggie thought, since he was starting to care for her. And that wasn't good when you had enough problems at home. Not to mention another woman he couldn't seem to stay away from.

James had come a long way with grooming and self-care but still struggled with a few daily tasks. Although Reggie didn't know him before the stroke, it was apparent that James still had some residual cognitive deficits and weaknesses from the stroke, as well as vision impairment.

Although this black man in his fifties was nothing like Reggie's six year-old daughter, he couldn't help comparing the two. Today, James got angry out of frustration and lashed out at Reggie. Simply projecting his anger, that was all it was. His frustration with the world, his stroke, the fact that he had to take a hiatus from teaching, his divorce – it all came crashing down on James at once.

It wasn't the first time Reggie witnessed a client have a breakdown. It was like he could physically see it happening. James' bitterness and resentment were almost palpable.

"Screw you, Reggie," James said, pointing his finger shakily. "You don't know what it's like."

Reggie wanted to tell him to kick rocks, to eat shit. But he would lose his job. And he felt for James. So Reggie remained silent. He quietly sat down on a kitchen chair and, placing his hands on the table, interlocked his fingers. James stared at Reggie for a moment then also took a seat. He struggled with pulling the chair out a bit, and Reggie let him struggle.

Once he was finally seated, James gently leaned his cane on the table next to him. "Man, I'm sorry Reggie. I shouldn't... I shouldn't have said that."

Reggie nodded slowly. "I know. And I know you didn't mean it. I get it, you're pissed at the world. But I'm not your punching bag, my man. I'm here to help you, James."

"That I know," James retorted, putting his palms up in the air. "What can I say? I'm angry."

"That I know," Reggie echoed. His eyes found the clock above the doorway. He had some time to spare. "James, you are my last stop for the day. Do you care if I tell you a story? I'll make you a sandwich while I talk."

James contemplated this for a beat, then nodded. "Sure. Okay, thanks. I could use a bite to eat."

Reggie made James a ham and cheese sandwich. He peeled an orange and put chips on the side, then poured James a glass of tea. And he began to talk. Reggie told James about Kate and their children. He knew about them; naturally

Reggie had mentioned that he had a family in conversation. But after Reggie set the plate and glass down in front of James, Reggie sat back down and began to talk about Paige's illness and the cat dying. James listened intently while he ate.

James listened while Reggie told him about Paige's cognitive struggles and how she was behind the other students at school. How her teacher suggested holding Paige back in the first-grade but that Kate adamantly refused. Reggie told James about how he continually compared Paige with Parker when he was the same age. How she wasn't hitting milestones like she should. How she had difficulty walking fast, let alone running.

Kate and Reggie continuously argued over whether or not to tell the kids about the incident when they got older. Naturally, Parker knew that Paige had been sick and was in the hospital, but he was a little too young to remember what it was all about.

Paige had no recollection of it since she was just a toddler. Reggie leaned toward explaining it to Paige when she got older, as it may deem important down the road. Especially when it came to school and telling her doctor. Kate adamantly refused, saying she didn't want Paige to remember the accident or risk traumatizing her further. It was as if Kate wanted to make sure she never gained any memories of what had really happened or something like that.

James finished eating and took a long sip of tea. "Man, Reggie. I'm sorry to hear that. It sounds like your family has been through a lot."

"Yeah, it's been tough at times. But Paige is resilient. It's

Kate and I who are still struggling. Honestly, I'm surprised our marriage survived."

James nodded slowly, scratching his forehead. "Has it?" he asked.

"What's that?" Reggie asked, leaning back in his chair.

James tilted his head to the side and shrugged. "Your marriage, has it 'survived', as you said?"

Reggie thought about that for a moment and frowned. *What did this guy know about my marriage?*

Apparently, a hell of a lot, Reggie realized.

"Yes and no, I guess," he finally said. "Don't get me wrong, I love my wife. And I love my kids more than anything. But... I'd say I am taking it day by day."

"And Kate? What would she say?"

"Okay... so who's helping who now?" he joked, standing and taking James' plate to the sink.

"I'm being serious," James responded. "You've done so much for me over these past several months, Reggie. And I feel terrible for yelling like I did earlier. It was unbecoming and for that I apologize. Leave the plate."

Reggie was already washing James' plate in the sink. "It's fine," he said. "I better get going. Same time Wednesday?"

James hesitated as if he wanted to say something more, but he didn't. "Same time Wednesday."

After Reggie got settled into his car, he pulled out his cell phone from his back pocket. He had seven text messages and three missed phone calls.

It was going to be a long night.

CHAPTER 25
CORA

September 30, 2019 – Monday

It was a crisp morning, but the sun was out. Cora always took it as a good sign when the sun came peeking out from behind those (sometimes relentless) Pennsylvania clouds, those bastards. Nearly killed Cora's tiger flowers this year.

Cora had been keeping a close eye on the Beckford house and had seen Reggie with the cat that morning. She saw him holding it, cradling the skinny, tan-colored thing like a small child. Cora had to admit, she felt terrible when she had seen Arlo taking the cat out to his vehicle not long after Kate and the kids had left. It was wrapped up in a towel, but Cora knew it had to be the cat. Thank goodness Cora found Charlie's good binoculars because she wouldn't have been able to see all of this funny business without them.

Hmm. Charlie.

Cora guessed, simply put, she had way too much time on her hands now that Charlie was gone. She wished the girls would come by more often. Maybe then Cora wouldn't have so much time to stew. And ponder things. And observe her neighbors.

After she watched the whole clan leave, Cora headed outside and did her rounds – pulled weeds, watered the garden, inspected the area for unwanted critters. Then Cora walked down to the lake with a mug of coffee and a tote bag that held her gardening book and a crossword puzzle book that the grandkids gave her for her birthday.

Cora hated crosswords; she didn't like anything that made her feel, oh... *stupid*. Nevertheless she attempted to work on it because her granddaughters bought it for her. So she sat, staring at the lake, missing her Charlie.

Quite quickly, Cora had become fond of Arlo. Alas, he was married. To that much younger woman, no less! But she hadn't been around, and Arlo broke his arm. *Strange, that whole situation,* Cora mused. But then, they were a strange family. Cora remembered Arlo mentioning that his wife was out of town, but what wife wouldn't come home if her husband got hurt? Maybe the marriage was in trouble. *Maybe*, Cora thought, *I should mind my own business.*

But why start now?

CHAPTER 26
ARLO

September 30, 2019 – Monday

Natasha was on her way home. Home! I didn't even care if she had bad news to tell me, I just wanted to see my beautiful wife. I missed her so much. Even if Kate was right and Natasha was having an affair, I didn't care. All that mattered was that she was coming home.

I got the mail and went through it all, even though it was a difficult task with the cast. Just a bunch of bills.

I wiped down the kitchen counters and made our bed (I still hadn't made it since the night I fell down the steps). It was too late to attempt to wash a load of laundry, so it was a good thing there wasn't much there. My dirty clothes were still at Kate and Reggie's anyway.

I sprayed air freshener that I found under the sink and put clean hand towels in both the master and guest bathrooms. Ridiculous, yes. I knew it sounded ridiculous. But my wife liked things tidy and in their place. And, maybe more to the point, I couldn't sit still.

I checked the digital clock on the stove; it was close to four o'clock. I'd spoken to Natasha about an hour ago. She should be home any minute.

When I heard a car pull into the driveway, I saw Natasha and I went outside on the deck to meet her. She looked beautiful as ever; although, I could tell, even from a distance, that she was sad. Natasha's complexion was spotty, her mascara smudged. She'd been crying.

A bad sign.

"No, don't come down," she yelled up to me. "I don't need you falling again!" Natasha smirked and we both began to laugh. *Good sign.*

Natasha trotted up the stairs and gave me a long, tight squeeze. It had been nearly two weeks since I'd seen my wife – the longest we'd gone without seeing each other since we'd met.

She was smaller than I was – and much shorter. I wrapped my arms around Natasha (as best I could) and noticed she'd lost weight. I could feel her ribs on her back, even underneath her thick sweater.

"My God, I missed you."

"I know, I know," she said. "I'm so sorry. I'm sorry, Arlo."

I kissed the top of her forehead, and she smiled and began to cry. "Let's go inside. I'm cold."

"Okay."

I made her a cup of hot tea, and we sat down on opposite ends of the couch, facing each other.

Natasha inched closer and took my left hand in both of

hers. She smiled and leaned in closer to me. It was the way she'd always been, always able to draw me in intrinsically.

"Natasha, sweetheart. I don't know what I did to make you leave, but whatever it is, I'll fix it," I said. "I don't want to live without you."

Please don't say there's someone else.

Please don't say you're leaving me forever.

She rubbed my arm with one hand, while squeezing my fingers with her other hand. "Arlo..."

"Please. Before you say anything else. Just know that I'm okay. I had a minor concussion, and the doctor is confident my arm will heal just fine. I've been doing all right without you, at least physically. But emotionally, I'm a wreck. I miss you..."

"Arlo..."

"There's no one else, is there?" I finally brought myself to ask. "Are you seeing someone else?"

"What? No, I..."

"You can tell me if there is," I prompted.

"No, Arlo. No, there is *no one* else," Natasha retorted. Taking her hands off of my arm, she wiped a few stray tears from her cheeks that escaped from her eyes. "I'm sick, love. I'm very sick."

Oh, God.

"Oh, no."

She was trying to hold back tears. "I'm very sick."

Then I knew. Natasha didn't have to say anything else; I already knew. After all, it's what killed her mother and sister.

Natasha went on. "I went to New Jersey for some testing. I'd gone to a few appointments before our last vacation, but when I knew for sure, well... I needed to stay in the city with Joyce, so I could go back and forth to these appointments. I didn't want to worry you unnecessarily..."

Huntington's Disease.

I should have known; I'd done my research when Natasha initially told me nearly a decade ago. Huntington's Disease is an inherited brain disorder that usually develops in a person's thirties or forties. I was big on research, as I've said, and I remembered certain phrases.

Cognitive disorders.

Physical decline.

Mental decline.

No cure.

Progressive breakdown of nerve cells in the brain.

Genetic. A single defective gene.

No cure.

Treatable. Medication, therapy.

No cure.

No cure.

She'd started to show signs. Anxiety, irritability, forgetfulness, difficulty concentrating. I'd known and yet had been oblivious to them. Or maybe I just didn't want to believe that it could happen to her. She inherited the gene, so what did I think, that she was immune? As if my wife's mother and sister were going to get sick and die, but she wouldn't? Couldn't?

I wanted to ask my wife what she was going to do next; what were our next steps? Was it treatable?

But Natasha was still crying, tears came faster until they weren't really tears at all. Just streams down the sides of her face. The skin around her eyes was an unforgiving red. The tears fell so fast she wasn't even attempting to wipe them away anymore. So I just took her in my arms, well at least the good arm, and held her while she sobbed.

"I'm so sorry, Arlo. I know I shouldn't have kept all of this from you, but you already lost one wife," Natasha said into my shoulder, her arms wrapped tightly around my neck. "I don't know if I can bear the thought of you watching me wither away. You don't deserve that."

It was true. I'd been selfish in thinking that me, pushing seventy, would die way before Natasha. Despite knowing her genetics, it never really occurred to me that I could possibly watch my wife, twenty-five years younger than me, go before me.

It was one thing to witness my first wife die – it had been a matter of minutes. Sure, that day haunted me for years to come. Still did, truthfully. And Sean and Kate had to see their mother pass away, which had made it all the more painful for all three of us.

Yet it was a moment in time. Celeste falling to the ground like a leaf and never getting back up. That was one thing.

But this, no. Natasha wouldn't suffer this alone. This illness would kill us both.

CHAPTER 27
KATE

September 30, 2019 – Monday

Reggie said nothing about the cat. Right before dinner, Parker asked where Baylor was when he didn't come to the food bowl with Banks and Gwynn. Reggie lied; he said he didn't know. Paige, who generally didn't care much about the cats, asked three times where Baylor was.

Kate told the kids she didn't know, either, which was the truth.

"He probably just wandered off, looking for a mouse or a chipmunk," Reggie said while he ate his spaghetti. "You know Baylor is the one who likes being outside the most. Always roaming the neighborhood."

Paige was playing with a meatball, rolling it around on her plate.

"Sweetheart, just eat it," Kate had to say at least half a dozen times, but Paige didn't listen. She just kept rolling the meatball around the noodles, like it was a damn hockey puck.

"I hope that old lady Mrs. Barnes didn't take him," Parker said. Kate thought he looked so cute with sauce on his cheek.

"What do you mean, 'Mrs. Barnes took him?'" Reggie asked.

"She yelled at me and Miles a few times when our football went in her yard. And she told me to keep the cats out of her garden."

"You never told me that," Kate replied, concerned. The fact that Cora would yell at her son agitated Kate. "Paige, sweetie. Just eat your dinner, please!"

Paige looked at Kate, but her expression was indecipherable. Reggie prompted his daughter, and Paige finally took a bite. Paige listened to Reggie better than Kate, which always bothered Kate.

Parker made a face. "Yes, I have, mom. I told you and dad a million times! But you two are always too busy *arguing* or paying attention to Paige to listen to *me*."

In all honesty, the boy was right. "That's not true."

"Whatever."

"Parker..."

"Mom, Miles just told me, like, two weeks ago that Mrs. Barnes yelled at him because he had Pippa on a walk, and she took a piss in her front yard. Miles said Mrs. Barnes came running outside in a purple bathrobe and screamed at him."

Kate frowned. "Don't say 'took a piss,' Parker."

"I never really saw Cora Barnes as a mean old lady," Reggie said, scratching his temple.

Kate could see the wheels turning in Reggie's head. He could blame the cat on Cora and then he wouldn't have to admit that he knew Baylor was dead. Nor would he have to admit he disposed of the cat and never told his family.

Kate knew that Reggie wasn't that kind of man. He was a liar, sure, and a cheater (weren't most men?). But he wasn't evil or cruel. Pinning a dead cat on an old lady, Reggie wouldn't do that. *Would he?*

"Hmmm. I don't know, Parker. It's not like we know Mrs. Barnes..." Kate began.

Reggie finally chimed in. "No, that's ridiculous. I can't imagine Mrs. Barnes killing a harmless animal. She's just an old widow. She wouldn't hurt a fly."

"I didn't say she killed him. I said she *took* him. Maybe she locked him in the basement," Parker surmised.

"Mrs. Barnes killed Baylor?" Paige asked, shocked, as if she hadn't been here for the entire conversation. She did that sometimes, blocked the family out and then all of a sudden, it was like she was back in reality. She'd lose five, ten minutes at a time. God only knew where her mind went.

Parker went on. "Yeah, like she's torturing Baylor or something. Remember a few summers ago when Miles' turtle went missing?"

"No, sweetheart. Nobody killed Baylor," Kate said to Paige, patting her arm.

"Okay, listen," Reggie said sternly. "Mrs. Barnes is not hoarding neighborhood pets and torturing them in her basement. Parker, enough with the true crime bull... stuff."

Parker rolled his eyes and grinned. "Okay, okay! May I be excused?"

Reggie peered over at Parker, assessing his plate. "Yes. But put your things in the sink. Then get ready for practice."

"Okay." Parker picked up his plate and glass and left the

room. Kate could hear him put his things in the sink. Then she heard him run up the steps and slam his door.

Reggie gave her a look and shrugged. Kate ignored it; she was too angry to be his ally at the moment.

Paige looked from her dad to her mom. "Can I go too?"

Kate sighed. Paige would be starving in an hour and want anything to eat but spaghetti and meatballs. "Sure. Same as your brother, put your plate and cup in the sink. Then pick out pajamas. You need a bath tonight."

Paige nodded and left the room, without taking her plate or glass.

Kate thought Reggie was going to yell after her, but he didn't. Kate didn't have the energy either. The two finished their dinner in silence.

After Reggie took Parker to basketball practice, Kate gave Paige a bath and then cuddled with her on the couch. She read Paige a story (she wasn't reading yet), and then they watched an episode of her favorite cartoon. It was about a mouse family that lived at the beach, which was just about the stupidest thing Kate had ever seen. But what did she know? It made Paige laugh and it wasn't violent, so Kate let her watch it. She was not dying on that hill.

Kate put Paige to bed before the boys got back, so she could lie down in her room and relax. She attempted meditating, using an app on her phone that a friend recommended. But Kate couldn't focus, so she retrieved two pills from the bottle in her vanity drawer and took them with a half glass of wine. Then, for the hell of it, Kate finished the glass.

Arlo called earlier in the evening, while Kate and the kids

were driving home. Arlo told her that he was staying at his house tonight. Natasha had come home.

Kate knew that he did it on purpose too,. Arlo called while she was in the car with Parker and Paige, hoping that she either wouldn't answer or, if she did, wouldn't nag him while in the car with the kids.

And he was right.

"Okay, great Dad. I'll talk to you tomorrow, hopefully." That's all she'd said. Kate didn't ask why Natasha initially left or why she decided to finally come home; although, she wanted to. But again, it wasn't the right time.

And because she was angrier yet at Reggie. And because, earlier in the day, her student Josie confirmed what Kate had already suspected. That Reggie was seeing Tara again. *A man had been around*, Josie told Kate. Not knowing that she was telling Kate that *her husband* had been around.

Recently, Reggie has been coming home later and later. He kept his cell phone in his pocket. He took it with him when he went to shower.

Rookie mistake, Reggie.

Kate knew that Reggie was sleeping with Tara three years ago when Lydia, a mutual friend, told her. Lydia was an aid at the elementary school and also Tara's cousin. There was some family drama, and, apparently, Lydia and Tara had a falling out. Lydia confided in Kate that Tara slept with lots of men, and she targeted married men. One of those married men being Lydia's husband. Kate's Reggie being another.

Kate never confronted Reggie about the allegations. She chose to make calculated moves instead. And she didn't want to lose her family. Especially when Pagie became ill.

The affair eventually ended; Kate knew because things

went back to normal. Reggie started coming home on time again and had been more affectionate with her. This was just after Paige's illness, and Reggie was transformed once more into the doting family man that he once was. *So be it.*

But over the past two months, Kate knew Reggie was having an affair again. He was back to keeping his cell phone with him wherever he went and making excuses to go out in the evenings. He joined a fantasy football league, and he didn't really even care for the sport. He miraculously made friends with a few coworkers (he rarely saw them on a daily basis), and the guys started going out for wings and beer.

Unlikely he ever did any of those things.

Kate didn't know if Reggie was seeing Tara again or another woman, but she had vowed to find out. It became much easier when school was back in session in August, and Kate and the kids weren't home all day together.

It was customary for Kate to take her lunch break in school, just in case one of the kids needed her. But the week before her dad came to stay with them, Kate made it a point to tell Ms. Simpson one day that she needed to run an errand on her break. Kate said she might take longer than her allotted half-hour lunch. Ms. Simpson didn't look pleased but, then again, she wasn't Kate's boss so what was she going to do?

Since Reggie was an occupational therapist, he drove to clients' homes most of the day. He could be anywhere! And he was professional, never speaking of his clients by last name or location to his family.

But Kate already knew where Josie and her grandmother lived, she'd driven past it religiously three years earlier. The old brick house wasn't more than a few miles from the elementary school. Kate started there, hoping that maybe she'd catch a glimpse of Tara or Reggie or his car, at least. She didn't.

Kate tried again the next day, making an excuse and taking her lunch break a little later in the afternoon. No Reggie.

On the third day, Kate drove around to a few motels in the area. Still, she didn't find Reggie's old Mazda.

That Thursday, though, she got a lead. Reggie messaged Kate to say that a new client had been added last minute to his calendar and he planned to stop at the end of the day for a quick check-in and evaluation.

Bullshit, she thought.

Kate acted disappointed. She wasn't. This was the break Kate needed. She felt like an old gumshoe on the brink of cracking a big case.

After school, Kate gathered the kids in her Sienna and surprised them with an early dinner at McDonald's. Paige was thrilled because she could eat chicken nuggets for breakfast, lunch, and dinner, and Parker would live on milkshakes. Kate went through the drive-thru, and the kids ate in the car, something she rarely permitted. Distraction number one.

A few moments later, Kate casually mentioned needing to run a few errands and allowed the kids to play with their iPads in the car. Distraction number two.

Kate was not a big fan of excessive screen time, but she needed to keep the kids busy while she drove around. Finally, she saw Reggie's gray Mazda parked outside a rundown motel, conveniently situated behind a gas station and grocery store, on the far side of town. Kate would recognize her husband's car anywhere. It was particularly easy to spot because of the Pittsburgh Pirates bumper stickers. *Idiot.*

Kate made a U-turn, stopped for gas, drove past the motel again, went through the car wash, and guided the Toyota back past Reggie's car. The kids were still munching away in the backseat, their eyes glued to their screens.

After about thirty minutes, she spotted Tara. She was tall and lean with a pillow of dyed-blonde hair. She'd be pretty if she wasn't so trashy, Kate thought at the time. Druggies all had those same deep-set eyes and bad skin. Tara stepped out for a smoke, wearing a man's t-shirt (Reggie's shirt!) and cotton shorts.

Kate wasn't sure if Tara saw her, but Kate didn't think she did because Tara was looking at her phone. Kate wanted to wait around to see Reggie come out the door, but she didn't want to be spotted, and the kids were beginning to get restless. Parker had to pee from his large milkshake, and Paige was hot and wanted to go home to change. Not actually seeing Reggie didn't matter. She had her proof.

CHAPTER 28
ARLO

November 7, 2008 – Friday

The bar was called Blue's. It opened in the late nineties and was a place the locals frequented. Not many Poconos visitors knew about it, and staff and patrons alike seemed to appreciate this.

On our first date, Natasha and I exchanged several personal tidbits while we ate at the swanky restaurant she'd chosen. I mentioned my first wife died young, and I'd never remarried. Instead, I'd chosen to spend my time building my business and raising my two kids, who were now grown and out of the house. Natasha disclosed that she was married twice, and was currently going through a divorce from her second husband. We didn't go into much detail, and neither of us pried. We were both on good behavior as we munched on delicious, overpriced appetizers and drank red wine, neither of which I was necessarily a fan of. But Natasha was so amazing to talk to, I probably would have had a great time no matter where we'd gone or what I had to eat.

I thought about her a lot over the next week or so and, apparently, the feeling was mutual. We talked on the phone, and Natasha got me to send text messages, something I wasn't fond of but was used to because of Kate and Sean.

On a Thursday afternoon, I called Natasha and asked her if she liked to play pool or shoot darts, and she said she wasn't good at either.

"I like to bowl," she said.

"Do you, really?"

She gave an exasperated sigh that I could feel through the phone. "What, you think I can't bowl, Arlo?"

"No, it's not that. Not at all!" I declared in self-defense.

"What is it, then?"

I laughed a little. "You just don't seem like the type. I mean, you're too pretty to be a bowler."

"Arlo, that's sexist," Natasha reprimanded.

"Oh, shit, I'm sorry. I didn't mean for it to come out like that. I really didn't."

"Apology accepted. Now are you going to take me bowling so I can kick your ass, or what?"

How can a man turn down an offer like that?

So, that's how our second date had come to fruition. We played seven games and Natasha won six of them. After I admitted defeat, we walked to Blue's next door, which was connected to the bowling alley by a long walkway. I asked Natasha to pick a table while I got us drinks.

Blue, whose God-given name was Buford, was the owner and the bartender; although, he was not a very good one. Blue generally had a cook in the kitchen and a waitress or two in the bar, which was a good thing since Blue had zero sense of urgency.

Buford was nicknamed Blue after Forrest Gump's character Benjamin "Bubba" Buford Blue. Buford wasn't black, but he'd start talking about a subject and not shut the fuck up about it, like Bubba and his shrimp. Apparently, his friends initially started calling him Bubba but then it somehow turned into Blue. Local legend has it that, after a particularly wild night at a field party, Buford got especially drunk and puked some type of blue wine coolers on a girl's shoes. Buford always adamantly denied this story by saying the nickname was because he used to dye his hair blue as a teenager.

So who really knew?

But regardless, there you have it – Blue.

"Arlo, my man! How have you been?" Blue chuckled, a big hearty laugh. He set two napkins down in front of me. "I see you have a lady friend with you..." He let his sentence trail off to see if I'd take the bait.

"Yes, I do." I answered, smiling. "I'll take a Harp, please. And my friend will take a Yuengling."

"Ah, a local lover," Blue said, winking at me.

"Ha! Yes, I suppose. I'll start a tab."

"Sure thing, Arlo."

I didn't hand Blue a credit card because we knew each other well and he trusted me. Blue's father, who passed away from a heart attack a few years earlier, had been an employee of mine. With his hefty size and love of beer, fried food, and cigarettes, sadly Blue would probably follow in his old man's path.

Blue set both beer bottles down in front of me. "You gonna eat?"

I nodded and turned to see that Natasha had found us a

booth in the back. For a Friday evening, the place wasn't that crowded. She caught me looking her way and waved.

"Yeah, probably."

Blue handed me a menu. "I'll have Iris come over when she's back from her break."

"No rush," I said, tucking the menu under my arm. I picked up the beers and walked over toward Natasha.

I slid into the booth across from Natasha. She was wearing a black sweater and dark jeans. Her dark eyes pierced through her black-rimmed glasses and it felt as if she could see my thoughts. *I could just stare at her all night,* I remembered thinking.

I set the Yuengling down in front of her and the menu between us. I took a sip of my beer before placing it on a napkin on the table.

"Thank you," Natasha said, taking the bottle and drinking from it. She turned the menu, so it was facing her. "You hungry, Arlo?"

I shrugged. "I could eat."

"Same."

"I have to admit, I'm a little sore. I haven't bowled in quite a while," I chuckled. "You're really good."

Natasha laughed, too. "Thanks. My friends and I used to go bowling a lot in college. I was in a league for a while." There were a few seconds of silence, and then she spoke again, "You know, Arlo, I'm a lot younger than you."

I smiled. "Yes, I figured as much. How old do you think I am?"

Natasha tilted her head to one side and then the other, then tapped her lips a few times with her index finger. "Hmmm. I think you look like you're in your fifties..."

"Well, thank you –"

"... but you're retired. And you have two adult children, so I'm going to guess sixty-two, sixty-three?"

I frowned. "What, you think I'm that old?"

She shrugged and held her palms up then took another drink of beer. "I don't know. You're very handsome, Arlo. I'm not trying to offend you."

I was momentarily taken aback by this beautiful woman calling me handsome. No woman, other than my daughter, had said something nice about me, particularly my appearance, in quite a long time. "You're not far off. I'm fifty-eight," I corrected her.

"Well, see. I *wasn't* far off," Natasha said, taking a look at the menu then flipping it over.

"What about you?"

Natasha looked up at me and smiled. "Well, Arlo. I'll ask *you* now... how old do you think I am?"

I took a sip of beer and tipped the bottle toward her. "Touché. I'll say you're thirty-four, thirty-five if I had to guess. Which apparently, I do."

We both snickered and then Natasha nodded. "Dead on, I'll be thirty-five next month. I'm a Christmas baby."

I didn't reply right away because, frankly, I wasn't sure what to say. I knew Natasha was much younger than I was. Without knowing why, I wondered what my kids would think. My sisters and my friends, the few friends I had. And my parents, who weren't even alive any longer.

I was just about to answer Natasha when I was temporarily interrupted by our waitress, Iris, who also happened to be Blue's cousin.

"Hey, Arlo. Long time no see," Iris said as she appeared at our table. "How the hell are you?" She patted me on the shoulder and smiled at Natasha. "I hope I didn't keep you two waiting long. I called the babysitter to check on the kids."

Iris was my age but looked much older. Her gray hair was pulled up in a loose bun, and I noticed that her skin was dry and cracked. Like Blue, working in a bar late into the night, along with the heavy drinking and smoking and God knows what else will do that to a person.

"No problem," Natasha said.

"Iris, it's good to see you. This is Natasha."

"Hello, hon. Any friend of Arlo's is a friend of mine." Iris grinned, and I could see she was missing a few teeth.

"It's a pleasure to meet you too, Iris. I absolutely love your necklace," Natasha said and genuinely meant it. Even then, it was apparent that Natasha was the type of person who could talk to anyone and make them feel special.

Iris tugged at the four-leaf clover charm that hung on a silver chain around her neck. "Oh, this? Thanks, hon. It was a gift from my daughter." Iris grinned and kissed the clover and then let it drop to her chest. "What can I get for the two of you?"

Natasha looked over the menu, contemplating. "I'm deciding if I should be good or not…"

"Always better to be bad, right?" Iris joked, slapping her own thigh and grinning.

"True! Okay, I'll have a burger, medium rare. Everything on it, please. And fries."

"Perfect," Iris said, "Arlo?"

"I'll have the same," I responded, handing Iris the menu.

Iris walked away with a promise to bring us two more beers and our food shortly. When she was out of ear shot, Natasha leaned forward and looked at me and whispered, "She said she had to call home to check on the kids. Surely, she doesn't have little ones at home?"

I shrugged. "Her daughter, Mallory, had twin boys. I'd say they are four or five now. Iris takes care of them."

"Oh, okay," Natasha whispered. "So where's their mom?"

I took a quick sip from my bottle and finished my beer. I took a deep breath in and out. "Mallory? She killed herself."

"Oh, no! That's terrible."

"Yeah, it really was. Mallory was a beautiful girl, inside and out. Straight A student. Went to college. I can't remember what for, but she had a decent job. Then she met this guy, a real asshole, you know?"

Natasha nodded, "Yes. I know the type," she grinned. She had leaned in close to me, and I had her full attention. Natasha had that way about her; she made me feel like everything I said was the most important thing in the entire world.

"He was a deadbeat, couldn't hold a job. Anyway, he got Mallory into drugs. Then he got her pregnant and left."

"Classy."

"Yeah, I know." I turned toward the bar to make sure Iris wasn't nearby. "Mallory was really depressed after she had the boys. Started using again. I guess it all was just too much...."

Natasha held a napkin between her fingers and thumb, and was rolling it so it looked like a snake. I looked down, and she realized what she was doing. "Nervous habit," she said in the way of an explanation. "Wow, that's so sad."

"It is. Poor Iris has to be exhausted taking care of them. And her husband's disabled." I paused and shook my head. "The woman's got it rough. I couldn't imagine losing one of my kids like that."

"Sounds like it, poor thing." Natasha rolled the napkin up into a ball and tossed it off to the side of the table. "You seem to know a lot about the family…" It was more of a question than a statement.

"Funny thing," I replied. "My son Sean dated Mallory in high school. Before he came out, that is. But he and Mallory stayed friends for quite a long time afterwards."

"Okay, that makes sense. So, your son Sean is gay?"

"Yes. He has a boyfriend, Victor. I like him. He's way more outgoing than my son. They're a good match. You know how sometimes opposites complement each other?"

Natasha reached across the table and squeezed my hand. "Yes, I do, actually."

Her grip was soft but powerful, and I could feel the warmth she carried. I recalled when we first shook hands in the bank parking lot – when I knew Natasha was a fierce woman.

I was smitten with this person, who I barely knew but somehow knew well. She reminded me a lot of Celeste, who wasn't much older than Natasha when she died. Maybe that was why I was so drawn to Natasha.

Iris brought us another round of drinks and our food. We made small talk, discussing our families and how Natasha came to the United States as a little girl. I loved hearing her talk. When the bill came, Natasha argued with me about paying, but she gave in when I insisted.

"Fine, I will leave the tip then."

"Okay, deal," I stated, raising my palms in surrender.

I went to the bar to pay my tab while Natasha excused herself to use the ladies room before we left. I walked back over to the booth to grab my jacket and saw that she had left two one-hundred-dollar bills for Iris on the table, held in place by her empty Yuengling bottle.

I could have married her right then.

CHAPTER 29
REGGIE

September 30, 2019 – Monday

One of the phone messages was from Reggie's boss. The two others and all seven texts from yesterday had been from Tara. He couldn't ignore her any longer, she'd said, and meant it.

After Reggie left James' house, he sent Tara a quick text.

Sorry, just leaving work. I promise to call you tonight. xoxo

He was more than ready to get out of the house and take Parker to basketball practice Monday night. After Parker's coach started warm ups, Reggie stepped outside and dialed Tara's phone.

"Reggie, what the fuck?!"

"I'm sorry, babe. I really am," he said. "Listen, things have been so busy with work, and I forgot Parker had basketball tonight. Arlo's been staying with us, and it's just been a busy time."

"You keep making excuses… I'm getting really sick of it!"

Tara sounded high, and he knew she got very indignant when she was on something.

"Babe, listen. One of the cats died today, and it's a whole thing. The kids are really broken up about it. I just couldn't leave them. Plus, there was no way Kate would –"

"Kate! Jesus..." Tara hated when he said his wife's name, as if Reggie hadn't been with the woman for over a decade. As if *Kate* were the other woman, not her.

"I do have a family, Tara. You have a kid... you understand, right?"

But Reggie knew that Tara didn't understand. She was a shit mother. In fact, she was a shit human being. He didn't even know why he got pulled back in. Hell, Reggie didn't even know why he started seeing Tara in the first place or why he was talking to her now.

Reggie first met Tara when her mother Agnes had been assigned to him as a client. He'd started occupational therapy with Agnes three times a week and often went in the mornings when no one else was at the house. Agnes mentioned having a daughter and a granddaughter, but neither of which Reggie saw right away. Then one day, Agnes had to change their appointment time to the afternoon, and Reggie finally met her granddaughter, Josie. Reggie guessed the girl to be around Parker's age at the time – in kindergarten or first grade. Tara dropped Josie off and left. That was it. No small talk with Agnes. No goodbye hug or kiss for Josie. Tara had eyed Reggie cautiously, even after he'd introduced himself as Agnes' therapist.

Reggie had hated her immediately.

All the more reason to sleep with her, he'd figured. There was no possibility of getting attached. And, from what

Reggie had gathered between the lines in Agnes' stories, he could tell that Tara was the kind of woman who got around. They could do as they pleased and move on.

Only Tara would come in and out of Reggie's life for the next three and a half years, and not because he necessarily wanted her to. They were drawn to each other in that disgusting way that people enjoyed toxic relationships. And she held their relationship over Reggie's head, something he hadn't expected.

It had started out as just sex, and that was practically all it ever had been. He didn't love Tara, far from it. But Reggie loved having sex with her. Looking back, Tara was someone he could turn to when things got difficult in his personal life. Being with her was an outlet. Initially, Tara didn't care about Reggie and would basically shove him off of her after they'd finished.

Tara was an addict and wasn't picky – pills, weed, coke, booze. Whatever she could get her hands on. And, like most addicts, she didn't have much in the way of money or resources. Yet, she still found a way to get by.

Agnes only allowed Tara at her house because of Josie, and, even then, Agnes ended up kicking her out rather frequently. (Not that Reggie blamed Agnes, the poor woman didn't deserve a terrible daughter like Tara.) So, when she wasn't at her mother's place, Tara slept wherever and with whomever she could.

Sometimes after work, Reggie would tell Kate that he needed to run errands but actually had stopped at the store earlier in the day. He would run out and meet Tara at a motel that he paid for. They'd have sex then he'd go back home with the bags of stuff he had hidden in the trunk. The receipt was *always* misplaced so Kate couldn't check the time stamp.

At times, he thought Kate was catching on, so Reggie would try to cool it with Tara. Tara would get mad, threatening to tell Kate about the affair. So Reggie would have to give her money for food or booze, meet up for a quick screw, put her up in a motel.

Anything to shut her up.

"Yeah, whatever Reggie. So one of your cats died... how come?" She was slurring her words now.

"Baylor. He was old... I dunno. Natural causes, I suppose," he lied.

It was like she was talking in slow motion, about to fall asleep. "When can I see you? And don't fucking... don't fucking tell me you *don't know*."

"This week, I swear. Listen, I'm sorry but I have to go now. I'll call you tomorrow."

She was suddenly calmer, sweeter. "Okay, Reggie. But you better... please. I miss you."

He rubbed his eyes with the palm of his hand then reluctantly asked, "You have a place to stay tonight?"

"I'm with Cam." *Her dealer.* Tara would stay with Cam often, trading sex for drugs and a place to sleep. "He said I could stay here but only for a night or two."

Reggie hung up with Tara, with the promise to call her the next day.

What am I doing, Reggie thought. *And why in the actual hell do I let this go on?*

Reggie and Kate had their share of problems, like any couple. Things were bad for a while after they had Parker. Kate's postpartum depression was severe and sometimes

Reggie couldn't even stomach coming home from work. Kate would fight with him about the smallest things – a cup left out or a towel not folded properly. The next minute, she'd be in tears and telling Reggie how much she loved him and Parker. He never knew which version of Kate he was going to get when he walked in the door.

Kate was on an emotional roller coaster, which only got worse after she became pregnant with Paige. Her depression was worse the second time around, and Reggie found himself needing an escape.

He had slept with a few women before Tara, most of them one night stands. Kate was always so tired between work and two little kids; she'd hardly notice when Reggie was gone longer than expected.

Tara was the first woman that Reggie had been seeing consistently. And it had gone on far too long.

Just when Reggie had decided that he needed to end things with Tara, Paige had gotten sick. The whole event had left the family devastated and well, even though he did cool things off with Tara for a while, Reggie was drawn back to her.

So why not just end it with Tara for good? If Kate ever got wind of the affair, he could probably talk his way out of it; Tara was a drunk and completely unreliable. *Who would believe her over me? Why not just roll the dice and see if Tara would ever go to Kate?*

Because Reggie couldn't risk it. Because he loved his wife. But mostly because he was scared of what she'd do.

CHAPTER 30
KATE

October 1, 2019 – Tuesday

"I talked to Dad last night," Sean told Kate over the phone. It was noon, and Sean said that he hoped to catch Kate on her lunch break.

Kate paused. "Yeah?"

"Sounds like you already know..." he hesitated, hoping his sister would fill in the empty space.

She didn't. Kate knew what Sean was thinking. *Ugh, Kate. Always so hard to deal with. Always so... temperamental.*

Kate knew what her brother, the successful child, thought of her. Sean, the stable, level-headed one. The sane one. "Is this a bad time, Kate? I thought maybe you were on your break."

"No, I'm not. But I'm not really busy either," she said, trying to sound casual. "Just filling out some monthly forms for admin. What do you want, Sean?"

Her brother breathed heavily. He regretted he called; she

knew. "Okay. So you know that Natasha is back home with Dad, right?"

"Yep," Kate replied sharply. "He called me yesterday to tell me. We were driving home from school, so I couldn't really say much with Parker and Paige in the car, now, could I? He didn't come back to the house last night. I'm assuming they fucked like rabbits all night."

"Damn it, Kate. You don't have to be so... crude." She giggled. "Sorry, yeah that's a gross thought. Okay. So, you talked to Dad... what did he have to say?"

"Just that Natasha had come home, and they talked but still had lots to sort out. But... well, now just between us, okay?"

"Sure," Kate's tone was noncommittal.

"*Kate*... I mean it."

"Okay, yes. Sorry, Sean. Brother-sister bond. Just between us." Even though Sean couldn't see her, Kate zipped her lips and tucked the "key" behind her right ear, like she did when they were kids.

Tucked the key away, never threw it away.

"Well, you know how last week Victor had said he had lunch with Natasha?" Sean asked.

"If I remember correctly, you – in your drunken state – blurted it out. But yes, I recall."

"So when they went to lunch, Natasha confided in Victor that she was sick, and that is why she left. She didn't want to hurt Dad. Rather she didn't want to worry him unnecessarily until she knew how bad it was."

"How noble of her."

"C'mon, don't be so hard on Natasha," Sean said with a

lengthy groan. Kate could picture her brother standing up to stretch. "She's been through a lot, Kate."

"So has our father, Sean. He's nearly *seventy* years old. Unexpectedly lost his first wife, our mother. Or don't you remember?" Kate was getting angry. *How dare he stick up for that woman?!*

"How the hell did we grow up in the same house, Kate? How can you be so... I don't know... cruel?"

"Oh, shut up, Sean. I wished you'd stop trying to always be the peacemaker. You're dad's favorite, Natasha's favorite. Why do you have to be so... so damn perfect all of the time?!"

Kate's temper had gotten the best of her. It didn't take much for her to get upset lately. She'd talked to her family doctor about it, the one who prescribed her medication. She'd seen Dr. Terry for well over a decade, before she had children. He knew that her mother had died when Kate was young. He'd strongly suggested she seek therapy for her anger issues and resentment toward, well, everything.

Her brother had no idea what it was like for her, growing up without their mother. Her dad tried, but there was no one to teach her how to put makeup on or give her advice about boys. When Kate was eleven and got her period for the first time, she had to go to her grandmother and ask her to buy pads. No way Kate would have asked her dad – she would have died from sheer embarrassment. A friend at school told Kate she couldn't wear pads when she went swimming. So, about a year later, when they visited her dad's younger sister, Aunt Faye, Kate summoned the courage to ask her how to use tampons.

In many ways, Kate was still that little girl in the light

yellow dress who watched her mother fall down in front of her. Fall down and never get back up.

"You know what? It was a mistake to try and have a normal, adult conversation with you, Kate. You really are a piece of work. Not everything is about you."

"Fuck off, Sean," she said and hung up the phone.

CHAPTER 31
CORA

October 1, 2019 – Tuesday

Something bothered Cora when she was at the lake earlier in the day, and she couldn't quite shake it. She couldn't stand trying to finish that darn crossword puzzle, so she put it back in her bag. Cora noticed she still had the gardening book in her tote; she pulled the book out and set it on her lap.

Cora sat, watching the sun glisten off of the lake. She listened to the young kids running around at the playground behind her as their mothers warned them to stay close by. Ever so protective, even in this quiet little town. Cora observed people as they ate their lunches and looked at their phones. Most didn't even notice her watching them. And Cora was a watcher, indeed. She wouldn't consider herself a voyeur, more of an observer. Yes, a *keen observer*, she reasoned.

But mostly, she thought of Charlie. Cora and her husband had been married for nearly forty years when he died. Late at night, before bed, she'd talk to Charlie and tell him all of the good things that he was missing. Especially with their granddaughters, who were such a joy to be around. Charlie wouldn't believe how big they were all getting. All beautiful and smart, like their mother.

Cora missed Charlie terribly. Although she knew that she'd likely never get remarried, recently Cora hoped that maybe she'd find a companion – to at least have dinner with or accompany her to the theater every now and again. Sure, she had her daughter and her girlfriends, but it just wasn't the same. Arlo was the first man Cora had been attracted to since Charlie passed. Arlo would have been a potential prospect, but of course, he was married. To a beautiful, younger woman, no less. Cora still felt like something was off, and then she remembered a small tidbit from a few days earlier. The first time Cora met Arlo, she had that same book with her... the one Cora's granddaughters bought for her birthday. Arlo mentioned that is daughter Kate had that very same book. Her daughter said that the girls picked it up in town, at that small, family-owned bookstore near the diner.

The Beckfords didn't grow much of anything in their yard but weeds. The only flowers they had were some daffodils, which Cora swore she saw the kids plant with *Reggie*, not Kate. Cora could go on for days about the fact that it was May at the time... and everyone knew that you planted daffodil bulbs in autumn!

So, why Kate's interest in the gardening book?

Cora thought about her own flower garden – all of her daffodils, with their fresh cream colors, dazzling yellows and oranges. Most people didn't know that daffodils were poisonous, but the bulb was the most poisonous part, and who's going to eat the bulb? And, oh! – her gorgeous, sun-loving butterfly bushes! Cora's friend Winnie was so envious of her Miss Rubys, with their vibrant pink color.

"Cora, your butterfly bushes are so beautiful!" Winnie exclaimed last time she visited.

"Well, thank you," she'd responded. But really, Cora wanted to say, *I know they are, Winnie. I take care of my precious flowers, unlike you.* Winnie let her dogs run around in the backyard and dig in the dirt, and, for heaven's sake, the one liked to do his business in her flower garden. *Unbelievable!*

Cora's Miss Mollys were just as gorgeous as their sisters, and their deep bluish-purple color blended perfectly with the dark pinks from the Miss Rubys.

The hydrangea shrubs were one of her favorites, with their luscious pink, blue, green, and violet blooms. Cora planted them on the far-right side of her property, along the fence. Since hydrangeas needed partial shade, she always kept them close to the property line since her neighbor Maxine had two large maples that shaded that corner of the yard.

For the azaleas, Cora went with the late season variety, which bloomed midsummer well into September, sometimes October. Along with the hydrangeas, the azaleas were Cora's other favorites – radiant pinks and oranges, yellows and reds. And, like her hydrangeas, the azaleas needed about six hours of sun each day. Not too much, however, or they'd dehydrate. Because of the need for partial shade, the two beauties were planted side by side.

Cora sighed. She put so much effort into her flowers and her neighbor didn't know anything about gardening!

So, what was really going on with Kate Beckford?

Cora remembered it was August and just before Charlie died – he was very sick at the time – when she noticed that some of her beautiful hydrangeas and azaleas were damaged. Her daffodils, too. Any other time Cora would have been livid, probably gone on a rampage to find out what neighbor kid had thrown their ball and ruined her gorgeous shrubs. It looked like someone had trampled right through them! Charlie had been so very sick then, and she very well couldn't have complained to him about her flowers.

He passed away about a week after that day.

"Come to think of it..." Cora found herself saying out loud, but not to anyone in particular.

Cora looked around and realized most of the people she'd been watching were still where they were moments ago. Only a few minutes had gone by, but it seemed like she'd been off in a daydream for hours.

Cora gathered her things and, as quickly as she could muster, loaded everything into her bag and headed home.

CHAPTER 32
ARLO

October 1, 2019 – Tuesday

Natasha and I spent the evening before in each other's arms. We talked, we cried... I just may have cried more than she did. She asked me about my fall and my time at Kate and Reggie's place. I didn't mention the argument I had with Kate, nor about meeting Cora at the lake. Although, in time, I knew I'd tell her about both. Maybe I'd tell her when we drove to my doctor's appointment. The irony was that my wife was taking me to the doctor when she was the one who was sick.

We finally got around to discussing her illness in depth. Ultimately, Huntington's Disease was fatal; although, people with the disease can live up to twenty-five years with it. The question was were they really living – or simply suffering through?

Natasha stayed with Joyce while she had brain imaging tests, a CT scan, and an MRI.

"The scans didn't show any significant shrinkage in my brain, but I'll have to go back for further testing," she explained, ever so calmly. "They want me to have a few other tests, to check my balance, hearing, muscle tone, reflexes... things like that."

"Okay," I said because I wasn't quite sure what else to say.

"They'll probably want to do tests over a period of time... to record my decline."

Her decline.

"Do you think we should move, get a place closer to the city?" I found myself asking.

Natasha hesitated. "No. No, I don't think that's necessary. Not yet at least."

"But we'd be closer to the doctor's. To Joyce, to Sean and Victor. To your dad," I offered.

Natasha mumbled something that was both noncommittal and nondescript.

"There's not much in the way of medical advancement here," I said, attempting some humor.

I was on my back, while Natasha lay on her side, her arm stretched across my stomach. She was scratching my side, something she did often when we laid like this. I smiled to myself; I had my wife back. Sick as she may be, as broken as we were, at least we were together.

"Does your dad know?"

"No. I wanted to tell you first. But Joyce knows. She's the only other person that knows, besides you..."

I nodded but, realizing that my wife couldn't see me in the dark, I added, "All right."

"I plan to call my dad tomorrow. Joyce said she can bring

him down to visit if he wants. Or we can visit him in the city. I'll see what he wants to do."

Natasha's father wasn't much older than me. We got along well, in spite of that awkward detail. He lived in a condo not far from Newark. He was in good shape but didn't drive much anymore.

"Can I ask you something else?"

"Of course, love."

Again, I hesitated, not wanting to upset Natasha or cause a fight. "You said no one else knows. But Victor told me that you were sick..."

Natasha ran her hand down my arm again and shook her head. "He knows that I'm sick, yes. But I didn't tell him what was wrong. You know that Victor and I are close."

"Closer than you are to your own husband?" I shot back then quickly regretted it, even though I meant it.

Natasha sat up abruptly, still calm. "No, of course not, Arlo. But I didn't know how to tell you, or when. Victor doesn't know what the issue is."

"Although I'm sure Victor could guess since it runs in your family."

"Well, yes. That's true..."

"What did he say when you told him?" I asked, also sitting up, propping myself up against my pillows.

She shrugged and gave me a half-hearted smile. "Well, naturally, that I should talk to you."

I kissed her, and she held me tightly. "I'm so, so sorry that you have to go through this," I whispered, my forehead resting on hers. "But I'm here for you. You're not alone."

Natasha whispered back, "I'm so, so sorry I didn't tell you sooner. And I'm sorry I left like I did."

We fell asleep in each other's arms and awoke just before nine o'clock. I made coffee and eggs, but Natasha declined both, saying she hadn't had much of an appetite. We planned to get groceries. I also suggested we talk to Reggie about having an occupational therapist come to the house. With Natasha's inevitable deterioration, it was best to develop a course of action and a plan to assist Natasha since my old ass wasn't going to be much help, especially with my arm as it was.

Natasha agreed to this and asked if I needed to pick up anything from Kate and Reggie's house. I told her I'd left everything I took there the day before, so I would need to go over and get my things. We agreed that it was best to wait until later in the afternoon to head over. I could pack up my things and then we could sit down with Kate and Reggie after they both got home from work. Again, Natasha didn't protest; although, I knew she wasn't wild about the idea of sitting down with Kate.

An hour later, we were showered and dressed.

"Ready to run to the store?" I asked.

"Yes, just let me find my glasses..." Natasha spun around, hastily looking for her eyeglasses. She searched in her purse and then the kitchen counter.

"Arlo, help me look, love. I can't find them anywhere!"

I realized – definitively, just then – what this disease was going to do to us. I hadn't noticed before, but from that moment on I would notice everything. The slightest slur in her speech, the tiniest stumble in my wife's step, the forgetfulness. The slow, yet steady, decline of this beautiful soul.

"They're... your glasses. Sweetheart, they're on your shirt," I said, smiling at her.

She gave me a quick laugh. "For crying out loud, ha!" Natasha unclipped her eyeglasses and placed them on her face. "Okay, let's go, love. I'll drive."

"Are you sure?"

"Yes, of course. I can drive. C'mon now." Natasha grabbed me by the hand. We walked out the sliding glass door and across the deck, descending the stairs I'd tumbled down not so long ago. Both of us stepped slower and more cautiously than we usually did.

"I can drive myself to my appointment tomorrow," I offered when we got to my vehicle.

Natasha spun around to look at me. "Nonsense, love. I want to drive my husband to see the doctor while I can still drive. Got it?"

CHAPTER 33
REGGIE

October 1, 2019 – Tuesday

"Who was that?" Tara inquired when Reggie walked back into the room. She was naked except for an off-white sheet that she had wrapped around her bottom half. Tara was lying on her stomach on the bed, rummaging through her bag.

"Work," he answered, taking a seat on the bed across from her.

Tara looked up at Reggie and rolled her eyes. She continued digging in her purse until she found a nondescript pill bottle. Tara glanced up at him for a beat. "You're lying," she said coarsely, twisting the cap off.

Reggie reached over to the nightstand between the two beds and picked up his watch, a gift from his grandfather when he graduated college. It was two-thirty. Claiming to have a flat tire, Reggie canceled his last two clients of the day.

He had to quit doing this. He had to quit calling off work. He had to stop seeing Tara.

"Tara..." he said, putting the watch on.

"Don't, Reggie. *Jesus*. I know when you're lying. Don't fuck with me, okay?" Tara leaned over close to the nightstand and carefully set three pills down. She used the bottom of the pill bottle to crush them until the pills were nothing but dust. "Was it *Kate*?"

"No. And please don't hound me." Reggie pulled his socks on then got up to find his tennis shoes. He sat back down on the bed to put them on.

Tara wasn't attractive, but she could have been. Her nice, round breasts rested on the edge of a pillow she had propped underneath her. She had long, slender legs and a firm ass. But Tara abused her body, and it showed in her face. *Always in the face*. Tara appeared worn, tired. She had that look that all alcoholics and addicts have, which you couldn't quite put your finger on, but you knew it just the same.

Reggie stood and retrieved his wallet from the nightstand.

Tara looked up at him. "Oh, so now you're leaving?"

"I gotta get home, Tara. I'll call you tomorrow, okay?" Reggie was practically pleading with her to take it easy on him, and he silently chastised himself for sounding like such a chump.

Tara flung the sheet off of her and sat back on the bed. Stretching out her torso and chest, Tara leaned back on her forearms, exposing her entire body to him. She shrugged, feigning indifference, then gently ran her fingers down her neck, past her breasts, over her stomach. "Fine, if you need to go..."

It was a test. She was testing him.

Reggie put his hands up in defense. "I really do. I'm sorry."

"Whatever, Reggie. Give me a couple of bucks?"

Reggie sighed then opened his wallet up, setting two twenty-dollar bills on the bed next to her.

Tara picked one of them up and rolled it between her fingers. She stuck one open end up a nostril and, using a finger to keep her other nostril closed, snorted the powdery white line on the dresser up her nose. "Thanks."

"Always a pleasure," Reggie answered, vowing that he really needed to end this. This time for real and for good.

Tara sat up once again. "You sure you need to go? We could order takeout, watch a movie. You know I hate being alone."

"You could visit Josie..."

Tara wiped her nose with the back of her hand. "Oh, come on, Reggie. You know Agnes hates me."

She hates you because you're a terrible mother. That's what he wanted to say but didn't.

Reggie hesitated for just a moment, considered staying. But then he finally replied, "I have to go. I'm going."

Tara went to say something else, but then stopped. "Fine," she said, wrapping herself up in the blanket again.

He sighed heavily. "Lock the door behind me, yeah?"

Tara nodded dismissively.

Reggie put his wallet in his back pocket and grabbed his keys from the dresser by the TV. He tossed Tara the remote control and left.

CHAPTER 34
KATE

October 1, 2019 – Tuesday

It was a beautiful afternoon, so Kate told Parker and Paige that she wanted them to play outside after they finished their homework. There was supposed to be a thunderstorm later on, and Kate wanted the kids to get some fresh air before then.

It didn't take Parker long to finish his work; the kid was a whiz at everything, especially math, like Kate.

Paige, on the other hand, only had one assignment where she had to add the vowel to three-letter words like dog, hen, and cow. Kate sat with Paige at the dining room table while she completed her homework. She was silently frustrated with the time and difficulty it took for Paige to complete one sheet. One fucking sheet.

When Paige was done, Kate instructed her to go outside with her brother. Kate stood and headed for the kitchen, but Paige just sat there and colored on the back of her notebook.

"Paige, go outside, please. Go play with Parker."

"Mommy... I don't want to," she whined.

"Why?" Kate asked, leaning in the doorway.

Paige looked out the window and back at Kate. "Miles is outside with Parker. They make fun of me when I try to keep up with them."

"Nonsense," Kate answered, even though she knew Paige was right. But she needed time to herself before she went completely nuts. "Paige, honey... fine. Go up to your room then. Okay?"

Paige wasn't looking at her mother; she was still coloring. She still held her crayons and pens in a fist, like a toddler. Kate tried breaking Paige of the habit and so did her teacher. Reggie said not to stress about it and that it would come with time. But, like most things with Paige, there was little progress, and Reggie wasn't much help.

"Can I help you with dinner? Please," she asked but with little conviction. Paige still hadn't looked up at Kate, even though Kate was staring at her.

"No, Paige. Go up to your room if you're not going to go outside."

"Fine!" Paige got up and shoved her notebook and homework into her backpack, which was now wrinkled. "I'll go outside," she added, as if on the verge of tears. Kate watched as Paige literally dragged her feet, the toes of her shoes scraping against the tile floor in the kitchen.

Once Paige went through the sunporch and Kate heard the screen door slam shut, she ran upstairs to change her clothes. She hurried into a pair of yoga pants and a tight t-shirt that read *Poconos is for Lovers*, a gag gift from a coworker at their Christmas party two years ago. Kate sat at her vanity and applied concealer and blush and powder. Then she took two pills from the drawer and swallowed them with water from the bathroom sink.

Kate hurried back downstairs and started on dinner. Her dad called earlier and said that he and Natasha would be stopping by later to get his belongings. Kate for *damn sure* wasn't happy about this. She wanted to have dinner ready before they came over. Kate decided to make pork chops because she knew that Natasha didn't care for them. So hopefully they wouldn't stay to eat.

Kate was getting potatoes from the pantry when her phone rang.

"Hi Reggie."

"Kate? Sorry I'm running late. I had to –"

"When will you be home? My dad is stopping over with my *stepmother*, and, apparently, they want to talk to both of us."

Reggie sighed heavily. "Oh? What about?"

"No clue."

He hesitated. "I have forms to turn in and I need to stop at the office –"

"No! No, Reggie," she snapped. "I need you home."

"I'll be home soon. The day just got away from me," he said, and Kate almost believed him.

She checked the time. "I'm making dinner, and they'll be here in less than an hour."

"Kate, I'm sorry. I'll be home as soon as I can."

"Whatever. Listen, I think we need to talk," she declared, as sternly as she could. "You've been gone a lot lately. I don't know. I'm... I'm just not happy about it."

Again, hesitation. "I know. Things have been tough lately. My caseload is ridiculous. We're short staffed. You know two people just quit, and Victoria is on maternity leave —"

"Reggie…"

"Okay, yes. We can talk tonight. I love you."

"Okay." Kate hung up the phone without saying she loved him too.

Kate poured herself a glass of wine and drank half of it in one long swig. She was going to need a few drinks to survive the evening. *Damn you, Reggie.*

CHAPTER 35
NATASHA

October 1, 2019 – Tuesday

The last thing I wanted to do was talk to Kate. The woman had never liked me, and now Arlo wanted me to tell her about my illness. I really didn't want Kate to see me vulnerable because I knew she would just relish in my pain. That was the type of person she was.

Arlo and I agreed to visit Sean and Victor in the next few days. That conversation would go way smoother than this one, I knew.

I drove the two of us over, and, although Arlo and I had a really good talk the night before, suddenly we were both at a loss for words. The car ride seemed to last for hours, but it had only been a few minutes. Arlo knew I didn't want to go, or at least he should have known. But I had agreed, reluctantly, because talking to Reggie seemed like a good idea. Although I hadn't told Arlo, Joyce and I had already discussed occupational therapy at length. My best friend was in a similar field, so she'd been able to give me sound advice.

The difference, however, was that Joyce lived an hour away, and Reggie would have first-hand knowledge of the therapists in our area.

Finally, I reached over and turned on Pandora and scanned aimlessly. I glanced over at Arlo, who was looking out the window and was unnaturally quiet.

"Got any requests?" I glanced over at Arlo and giggled.

Arlo turned toward me and smiled. "Hey-yo!" he said and we both chuckled quietly.

It was an inside joke that we had kept going since one of our first dates. We'd gone to dinner and were walking back to the car. There was a middle-aged man sharply dressed in a white tuxedo. He was playing the guitar and taking song requests. He was rather tall and had long, dark hair and a mustache. A young Bob Seger, Arlo had said at the time. If you threw a five- or ten-dollar bill in his guitar case, he'd play whatever you wanted. I walked past the man, but Arlo stopped to watch him. I doubled back and joined Arlo and linked my arm in his. A crowd had gathered around on that unusually cool evening, and Seger seemed to be enjoying the attention.

"Hey-yo! Got any requests?!" The man would shout out. And, for whatever reason – whether it be the atmosphere, the guitarist himself, or really just the randomness of it all – Arlo and I found it hilarious. We would often ask each other, "Got any requests?" offhandedly over the years.

"Fire Lake?" It was Arlo's favorite Bob Seger song.

I laughed. "You find it, love. I'm driving."

Things went back to normal after that, until we reached Row Point. "I don't know if I want to do this."

"What do you mean? Which part?"

"Any of it, love. I should have just stayed home. Let you come alone. I'm not ready," I answered, rolling my window down for some fresh air. "I have a bad feeling."

"Natasha, sweetheart. It will be fine. It's my family. They love you..."

I gave Arlo a sideways glance and frowned.

"Okay, okay. I'll clarify. Reggie and the kids *love* you. Kate, well... you know Kate."

Did I ever.

A few years back, when Parker was just a baby, the entire family went out for pizza for Sean's birthday. We were all drinking beer, and I asked the waitress for a couple waters for the table. Apparently, Kate took this as a personal jab at her alcohol consumption. She stood up and yelled at me, "You're not my mother!"

Keep in mind that Kate was thirty-one at the time. While shouting at me, Kate swung her arm and knocked over an entire pitcher of beer, which spilled all over the floor.

Victor, who also wasn't Kate's biggest fan, made the comment that I couldn't be Kate's mother because I wasn't old enough. Reggie and Sean both laughed hysterically, while Arlo and I visibly cringed. Kate grabbed Reggie's glass of beer and dumped it on Victor's head then stormed out of the restaurant, got in the car and drove home, which left Reggie with baby Parker and no car seat.

That was the type of person I was dealing with here.

CHAPTER 36
ARLO

October 1, 2019 – Tuesday

Natasha and I gathered my things from the garage apartment and put them in the back seat. Natasha sat in the vehicle and phoned her father while I did one final walk-through to make sure I'd grabbed everything. Not that it mattered much. I didn't bring anything of importance over to begin with – a week's worth of clothes, a couple of books, my favorite pair of boots.

I found myself again looking at that photo on the refrigerator that I was so enamored with a week ago. I still adored the picture of my family but was also somewhat resentful now. Natasha had taken the picture and, naturally, wasn't in it. But, looking back, that seemed to be the way things went – Natasha was generally the one who was in the background.

But why? She was my wife of ten years, and I was the elder in this family. Kate and her husband and Sean and his husband – they were always front and center. Why not my wife?

I wasn't the best dad, but I did a hell of a job with the cards I was dealt. I lost my first wife at a young age. And not only did I do the best I could for my two children, but I also built a damn empire and ran it for years until I was ready to retire.

I stood there, looking at that picture on the fridge. And I vowed that I would use all of my resources to do whatever it took to take care of my sick wife. She would not suffer. I had the money and the means, not to mention Natasha had plenty of her own wealth from her own family's business. If I had to, I would use every last dime to take care of my Natasha – the finest doctors, the best therapists, any medications or comforts she needed. I promised myself that I'd do whatever was necessary.

And I vowed to take better care of my grandchildren. Parker didn't need much; he was already a smart, athletic kid. And I spoiled them both rotten with ice cream and toys and trips. But Paige – my sweet granddaughter. Paige needed a better speech therapist and family doctor. We needed to finally find a good therapist for her. She needed more attention at school – possibly a private school with smaller classrooms. I'd allowed Kate and Reggie to let things go for too long. Sure, they were both in the medical profession, but they were not acting professionally. Not when it came to their own child. Not when it really mattered.

Before leaving, I walked over to the bookshelf next to the small linen closet and grabbed two books that I knew Reggie probably wouldn't notice. I figured I'd be spending a lot of time at home and at doctor's appointments over the next several weeks. Maybe months.

The first book I picked, *We Are the Ship: The Story of Negro League Baseball,* was written by Kadir Nelson and was geared toward children. Surely, it was up here in the apartment because Reggie probably already read it to the kids or Kate moved it, more likely. The second book was also geared toward teens and young adults. *The Forgotten Players: The Story of Black Baseball in America* was written in the early nineties by Robert Gardner and Dennis Shortelle. I surmised it was a gift from Reggie's grandfather, the biggest baseball nut there was. I set both books on the sofa.

I scanned the shelf and noted, in fact, most of the books were about baseball. Surely not something Kate would have read. Then I spotted that book on gardening, the same one Cora Barnes had with her when we first met at the lake. Sheepishly, I recalled feeling attracted to Cora almost immediately.

"Damnit," I said to no one and rubbed my eyes. Maybe it was just because Natasha had left and I didn't know why, but knowing now that my wife was sick, I felt a disgusting feeling in my gut. Knowing that my wife was suffering while I was chatting with another woman, well... it made me feel like a terrible husband.

Curiously, I took the gardening book off of the shelf and leafed through it. Several pages were dog-eared, but I couldn't see why. Neither my daughter nor my son-in-law had a green thumb and didn't take much interest in their yard. Odd, that book being here. I thought it might come in handy, so I took it, along with the two baseball ones and headed out the door.

I walked down the garage stairs very carefully – since I was carrying the books with my good arm, I couldn't hold the railing well. I looked up and saw Natasha leaning against the car. She had her arms crossed, and there was a faraway look in her eyes as she peered over at the house.

"Did you get to speak to your father?"

Natasha looked over at me as if she hadn't seen me coming toward her. "Oh! Yes, love. I did. I told him we could visit on Friday if that's fine with you."

"Sure thing. Maybe we could take him to lunch if you're feeling up to it..."

Natasha tapped her lips with her pointer finger.

"Of course. I want to tell him about, well... everything in person," she said, adjusting her glasses.

"Ready to go in? I see Reggie's not home yet," I made it a point of scanning the driveway. "He never parks in the garage."

"Not that he could. Have you seen the inside? It's full of junk," Natasha whispered and made a face that made me laugh.

"Yeah, there's no way they're fitting anything else in there!"

We both chuckled, and then I sighed heavily. "Well?"

Natasha hesitated as if contemplating running away. "Should we wait for Reggie?"

I shrugged, "I'm sure he'll be home any minute."

She rolled her eyes. "What's that?" Natasha asked, pointing to the books I still had in my arm.

I held them up to my chest. "I'm going to ask if I can borrow these. I thought maybe I'd have some time at home... anyway, I thought I could make you a flower bed."

"That's sweet, love. Thank you." Natasha leaned over and kissed me softly on the lips, then on my left cheek. "I'm so lucky to have you."

CHAPTER 37
KATE

October 1, 2019 – Tuesday

Parker was helping Kate set the table when they heard the screen door open. Paige was in the living room but quickly hopped up and scurried through the kitchen then yelled, "Pappy! Mommy, Pappy's here!"

It was a complete one-eighty from an hour ago, Kate thought, rolling her eyes. It was the most excitement Kate had seen from Paige all week.

She heard Paige out on the sun porch talking to her dad and Natasha. The girl was practically squealing with delight. "Nooni! I missed you!" Kate heard Natasha mumble something back, but couldn't make out what she said.

Nooni. My God, did Kate hate that they called her that. But, yes, she was their grandmother.

Step-grandmother to be accurate.

Parker and Kate went into the kitchen and practically ran into Paige, who was coming to get them. Arlo and Natasha were right behind her.

"Mommy, did you know Pappy and Nooni were coming for dinner?"

Kate took Paige by the hand and bent down to her level. "Yes, sweets, I did! I told you earlier. How exciting, right?"

Paige nodded enthusiastically.

"Now go on and wash up for dinner, okay?"

"Okay!" Paige turned around once more and gave both Pappy and *Nooni* a hug before floating out of the room. Kate heard Paige bound up the stairs behind them.

"Parker, you've gotten so tall!" Natasha said, feigning surprise. *Really?* She saw him less than a month ago. "You're going to be as tall as your dad or your grandpa."

Parker beamed. "You think so, Nooni?"

"I know so, yes. Here, stand back to back." Natasha took both Parker and Arlo by the arm and scooched them close together.

Arlo and Parker laughed as Natasha sized them up. "Parker! You don't have much farther to go. I bet you're taller than Pappy by the time you're twelve."

"Come now, Natasha. I don't think so!" Arlo retorted, pretending to be dismayed by this.

None of them had yet to acknowledge Kate, so she busied herself with taking food into the dining room. Paige was sitting at the table and was back to her usual, distant self.

"Paige, what do you want to drink?"

Paige was looking out the window. Kate had to say her name two more times before she finally got Paige's attention.

At last, Paige looked over. "Yeah?"

"Water or milk, honey?"

"Milk," Paige said, looking back out the window.

"What's got your attention out there?" Kate probed. "Paige?"

Paige didn't bother to look at her mother. "Nothing. I thought I saw someone."

Kate let her be and went back into the kitchen. Arlo gave her a hug and Natasha asked if she needed any help.

After Arlo and Kate's attempt at a warm reception, Kate vowed to be on her best behavior, and she intended to try and keep that promise. She really had.

"Actually, I'm good. Parker, go wash up, please."

"You got it!" Parker answered, always obliging. Kate turned her attention back to her dad and Natasha. "Just entertain the kids, I guess, until I get dinner on the table." She hesitated. "I'm not sure when Reggie will be home, so let's not wait for him..."

"Up to you," Arlo said. "Let me go see what these kids are up to."

Natasha followed Arlo into the dining room, and Kate watched them both go. She noticed that Natasha was thinner than usual, and pale. She looked tired. Although Kate wasn't a fan of her stepmother, Kate had to admit that Natasha was an attractive woman. However, her usually glowing skin and bright eyes... they just weren't there.

While they entertained the kids in the living room, Kate busied herself getting the pork chops and potatoes out of the oven and threw together a quick tomato and cucumber salad. She silently chastised herself for thinking that Natasha was having an affair. Seeing Natasha now, it was obvious to Kate that something was wrong with her – what that was, Kate wasn't sure. But it was apparent that Natasha was sick.

To make things even worse, Kate felt bad about the pork chops.

CHAPTER 38
NATASHA

October 1, 2019 – Tuesday

*F*ucking pork chops. Kate knew I didn't eat pork. Fortunately, I didn't have much of an appetite, so I nibbled on butter bread and tomato and cucumber salad, which Kate evidently threw together at the last minute. I could tell that the dressing hadn't had time to marinate, and the cucumbers were dry.

Gwynn, the family's loveable Calico, was under my feet. He was rubbing his head against my leg. For a moment, I wished I had a piece of meat on my plate to feed him. Kate never gave the cats table scraps, even though they begged relentlessly.

Sorry, Gwynn, you wouldn't like this salad either, buddy.

Clearly, there was tension with Kate and Reggie. He came rushing through the door just as the five of us started to eat. The look Kate gave him was wicked. She thought no one saw, but I caught a quick glimpse of her face. I wondered if Kate knew about Reggie's past infidelity, which was obvious to me, but surprisingly, Arlo seemed clueless to it. Every now and again, I'd hint around about Reggie's discretions, but Arlo never seemed to pick up on what I was trying to get at. So, after a while, I let it go.

Victor and I talked quite a bit on the phone, at least once a week, and messaged almost daily. And Victor told me that he and Sean had always been suspicious of Reggie having affairs, and they live an hour away!

"Sorry, I'm late!" Reggie announced as he took a seat next to me. "I was –"

"It's fine, Reggie," Kate quickly interrupted. "No one cares. Just sit down and eat."

Reggie scooped several large spoonfuls of potatoes onto his plate. "Well, I apologize, especially to you, Arlo and Natasha. I didn't know you were coming until this afternoon, but still... it was rude of me."

"Enough, Reggie. We get it. you were late. You're here now," Kate inserted.

She was stabbing at her pork chop like it was her husband and she was murdering him. But then, realizing her actions, Kate swiftly attempted to switch gears, which fooled no one. "I mean, I'm just glad you're home safe. Don't worry about it."

"It's really no problem, my man," Arlo said, always trying to keep the peace. "We plan on staying for a little while."

Reggie nodded and smiled. "Thanks." He then looked over at me and patted my arm gently, studying my face. "How are you, Natasha? It's been a while. Always nice to see you." Reggie's kind eyes seemed to see right through me.

I shrugged and forced a brief smile. "I'm hanging in

there, thanks." I put my hand over Reggie's for a second and squeezed it.

"Not hungry?" he asked, noticing that I didn't have much on my plate.

Immediately, Arlo spoke up. "Natasha doesn't like pork chops," he said and gave his daughter a quick look.

"Oh..." Reggie said, also looking over at Kate, who was busy cutting up Paige's pork chop. I'm sure Kate could feel all of the sets of eyes on her, but she chose not to acknowledge them.

"I'm... I mean, it's... fine," I said, taking a drink of ginger ale. "I haven't had much of an... what do you call it?"

"Appetite?" Reggie asked.

"Appetite. Yes. I haven't had much of an appetite lately." Awkward silence followed throughout the rest of dinner, except for meager attempts at small talks: Arlo asking the kids about school, Reggie bragging about Parker's basketball progress, and me mentioning the inevitable thunderstorm that was to occur in about an hour.

"Will you be okay driving home?" Kate asked Arlo pointedly. I'm sure she was still bitter that I returned home, and Arlo left her house without notice.

"Oh! We'll be fine." Arlo waved his hand as if brushing the whole thing off. "You know PA weather. It might not even rain."

"I don't know about that, Arlo. Did you see how... umm, dark it's gotten outside?" I added, pointing out the dining room window. "It usually doesn't get this dark for... oh, I don't know. Another hour or so?"

"I saw Mrs. Barnes outside," Paige said nonchalantly, pointing outside like I just had.

Reggie looked over at Paige, who was seated beside Kate. "Well, she is our neighbor, Sweetheart," he stated casually. "You probably did see her."

Arlo perked up. "Mrs. Barnes? As in Cora Barnes?"

"Yes, dad. She's our neighbor."

"Nooo, Mommy. She was in our yard. Back there," Paige said, aggressively directing her hand toward the window. "In our yard!"

Kate gave her daughter a quizzical look. "Paige, sweetie... you said you saw someone earlier, before dinner. Did you see Mrs. Barnes? Is that who you saw?"

Paige shook her head emphatically.

"Cora is the lady I ran into at the lake."

"We know dad," Kate added. "You said you two hit it off." Kate shot me a quick glance, which I refused to react to. Although I was now curious who this Cora lady was, I wouldn't dare question Arlo in front of Kate.

"Don't be dumb, Paige. She lives back there," Parker interjected, pointing a thumb behind him. "Mom, I'm done. Can I be excused?"

Kate told him he could, and asked Parker to put his plate in the kitchen sink. "Paige, why don't you go up to your room, too?"

"I don't want to. Can I watch T.V. downstairs?"

"Paige, listen to your mother," Reggie said calmly, but sternly. Paige frowned but did as she was told. Both kids came around the table and gave Arlo and me a hug before leaving the room.

"We'll come up and say goodbye before we leave, yeah?" I said, squeezing Paige's tiny hands in mine.

Paige nodded and, after a few seconds, I let her hands

slip out of mine. It was times like this I envied Kate for being a mother and felt sorry for myself for not having the chance to become one. I could imagine myself tucking little ones into bed and reading stories and kissing foreheads.

Moments later, I could hear the kids trotting up the stairs, Parker already informing Paige to stay out of his room while he played video games. Paige whined, and then I heard one door slam and then a second. All of a sudden, I felt trapped. Just the four adults with no children as a buffer.

CHAPTER 39
REGGIE

October 1, 2019 – Tuesday

Of all the women in Reggie's life – Kate, Tara, Paige, his mother, grandmother, coworkers – Natasha was one of the easiest to be around. Maybe because they weren't related by blood, nor had they ever been intimate. Maybe that made it, well... uncomplicated. Natasha, Victor, and Reggie were close – the motley crew of in-laws – only related by their love of the Callan clan.

Natasha was a strong woman, no bullshit. She was kind, unassuming yet unaffected. One of the most level-headed, intelligent people Reggie knew. But something was off, and Reggie could tell as soon as he walked into the dining room that evening and saw Natasha and Arlo seated with Kate and the kids.

After Parker and Paige were upstairs and getting settled in for the evening, Natasha and Arlo helped Reggie and Kate clean up. Kate barely looked at her husband, and, when she did, it was to give him a look that said she'd murder him if she had a sharp enough knife and a spare minute.

After the plates were in the dishwasher and the leftovers were in the fridge, the three of them settled into the living room, while Reggie got drinks. Arlo and Natasha sat on the love seat; Kate took the recliner. Reggie handed everyone their drinks – a beer for Arlo and himself, a glass of wine for Kate, more ginger ale for Natasha. Then he took a seat on the couch across from his father-in-law and Natasha.

Arlo cleared his throat. "I wanted to start out by saying thank you for letting me stay with you while I recovered," he said, tilting his head in the direction of his right arm, still in a cast.

Natasha sat up and patted Arlo on the leg. "I'm taking him to his appointment tomorrow..."

"Dad, of course you're always welcome here," Kate chimed in, "Right, Reggie?"

"Sure thing," Reggie assented. "But Arlo, you *know* that. You both have done so much for us. We'll return the favor anytime we can." Reggie motioned flippantly toward Arlo and Natasha, a gesture he knew was sure to piss Kate off as soon as he did it.

"I appreciate you both," Natasha added. "Watching over Arlo while I took care of some things for myself. I know Arlo always loves spending time with Parker and Paige when he can..." She paused and smiled sadly. "I had to take care of some personal things. Umm, I... unfortunately, I received some bad news recently and needed to sort things out..."

Kate jumped on that. "And not tell my dad?"

Natasha stiffened. "No. Well, yes, I didn't tell your dad.

Not at first. But, frankly, Kate..." Natasha paused to glance at Arlo and then Reggie, and then back to Kate. "Frankly, that's between Arlo and me. But anyway, I had my reasons," she stated, straightening up.

Good for you, Natasha. Good for you, Reggie thought.

Kate went to speak, but he stopped her. "Babe, please. Let her speak," Reggie tilted his head and gave his wife a sweet smile. "Okay... please?"

She gave in. "Yes. Yes, of course. I'm sorry, Natasha. It's just that I'm very defensive when it comes to my dad."

Natasha nodded, once again looking over at Arlo. Reggie noticed a subtle odd movement Natasha made with her hand, like she was tightening it into a fist, rapidly but only for a few moments. Reggie remembered that she'd done it twice at dinner too.

"Yes, I know. And I understand and respect that, Kate. I'm very close to my father, too. Maybe if you two will hear us out, you'll understand my secrecy over the past few weeks."

Kate sighed and nodded but didn't say anything.

"We're all ears. Please..." Reggie answered, gesturing with his palms up. They had the floor.

Natasha let Arlo do most of the talking. And thank goodness, because Kate was kind enough to let him do so. She might not have given Natasha the same courtesy.

Over the next fifteen minutes or so, Arlo told them about Natasha's Huntington's Disease diagnosis and what that meant for the two of them. It made sense, Reggie realized, the small but noticeable changes in Natasha. The weight loss, the difficulty finding the right words, the vague look of confusion, the involuntary hand movements.

Natasha mentioned that she had recently become quite forgetful, but her physical disabilities seemed to be what was progressing the fastest. The two of them asked Reggie dozens of questions about having an OT come out to the house – when should they start that process, how often would a therapist come to the house, who would Reggie recommend?

Reggie was tempted to offer his services, but Kate would probably have stabbed him right then and there. He could tell that Kate, the nurse, was already perturbed because he was the one being asked all of the questions and had all of the right answers and not her. For once.

So instead, Reggie suggested Natasha complete the necessary paperwork as soon as possible because sometimes those balls took time to get rolling.

"I'm willing to pay out of pocket, to get an occupational therapist to come out more often, if I need it," Natasha added.

He was unwilling to agree with Natasha that she might very well need more help if and when (probably when) her health declined. Reggie didn't want to upset Arlo or her unnecessarily. Plus, Natasha's mother and sister had had the disease, and she wasn't naïve; she already knew what lay ahead for her down the road.

"We can talk further about that," Reggie said. "But I think having someone from the agency come out to assess the house would be beneficial."

Arlo looked at Reggie curiously. "Assess our house?"

"Yeah. To look for potential safety concerns. I mean, we wouldn't want anyone else falling down the steps," Reggie joked.

Arlo chuckled. "Ah, you got me there, Reggie!"

Arlo, Natasha, and Reggie burst out into laughter, while Kate leaned back, folding her arms across her chest, like a child might when she was told she couldn't have ice cream.

Natasha, paying no attention to Kate, made a rolling motion with her hands, as if she was tumbling.

"Holy shit, I can't take it!" Reggie joked, practically choking on a drink of beer he was trying to swallow.

Kate sat perfectly still, watching the three of them, as if they were her elementary school students and she was their teacher, patiently waiting for them to shut up so she could get on with it.

"What's wrong?" Arlo finally asked, after they quieted down.

"I'm glad you all find this so fucking funny," Kate replied blankly. "I mean, my dad had a concussion, Reggie. Natasha is dying —"

"Kate, I'm not *dying*..." Natasha chimed in. "I'm sick, yes. In need of help? Yes, of course. But I'm... I'm not dead for God's sake."

"My father is going to be seventy soon, and now he's going to have to take care of *you*. It should be the other way around, *Nooni*."

Well, shit. Here we go, Reggie thought.

Arlo stood up abruptly. "Now wait a minute, Kate," he muttered, pointing a finger at her. "I am perfectly capable of taking care of myself and my wife."

Kate cleared her throat and laughed loudly. "You fell down the stairs, and your wife wasn't even there to take care of you. And now... now she needs *you*?! This is just rich. Real fucking rich."

Arlo started to pace back and forth between the love seat and the doorway to the kitchen.

Natasha pursed her lips and looked over at Arlo. She looked at Reggie; he didn't know what to say or do right then, and frankly, he didn't want to be caught in the middle of this shit storm. Reggie shook his head and lifted his shoulders. He hoped against hope that the two of them would just leave before things were said and there would be no going back.

Looking back at Kate, Natasha narrowed her eyes and finally – calmly and quietly – spoke. "Let's get this out in the open, once and for all... what the hell is your problem with me, Kate?"

"Okay, that's enough. We're going. C'mon, Natasha. Let's go. Reggie, you and I can talk another time," Arlo stammered, taking Natasha by the arm, offering to help her up.

"I'm fine, Arlo."

"Mom? Dad? What's going on?" It was Parker at the top of the steps. He was holding onto the railing and looked over and down at everyone.

"Nothing," Reggie answered. "Everything's fine, buddy. We're just talking."

"You're yelling. I heard you guys."

Reggie hesitated. "We were talking loudly. Adults do that sometimes. But everything's okay."

"I'll go up and tuck them both in," Kate said to no one in particular and walked past her husband briskly. "Come now, Parker. Go on back to your room. Did you and your sister brush your teeth? It's a school night after all." Kate scooted Parker back upstairs, and Reggie could hear her go into Paige's bedroom and chastise Paige for something or other.

"I need a smoke," Arlo mumbled and headed toward the kitchen. Reggie heard the refrigerator door open. Arlo was probably helping himself to another beer.

CHAPTER 40
ARLO

October 1, 2019 – Tuesday

I left Natasha inside with Reggie and walked across the driveway to my vehicle. I needed a cigar and a break from my family. I reached into the glovebox for a Montecristo and found my lighter in the console. Natasha wouldn't be happy with me, and I felt bad for that. But not bad enough not to smoke – at least in that moment.

Walking to the end of the driveway, near the sidewalk, I lit my cigar and took a few puffs. I laughed a little to myself, realizing that it hadn't become any easier to smoke with my arm in this cast. I thought that maybe I'd cut back on the cigars after my fall and the difficulty I had with simple, mundane tasks. But alas, I was still at it. The scar on my chest was fading, but my love for my Montecristos wasn't.

The street was quiet and dark. It was that strange time of evening before it was completely dark, but still – it was hard for me to see, even just a few feet in front of me. A few street lamps were on, and families were starting to turn on porch lights. A few bathroom lights were on – kids brushing their teeth before bed, no doubt. But, still, none of the light helped much.

I began to wonder about things I'd taken for granted recently, and I was sad. It was hard for a man of my age to admit that, but it was true. It was also true that Kate, despite her reprehensible delivery, was right. I loved Natasha very much, though deep down I didn't know if I was capable of taking care of her.

Hence, the need for professionals, I supposed. *We had the resources; we could make it work*, I thought.

I wandered around, making my way back over to the garage. I thought I'd heard a voice, a woman's voice, and I looked around aimlessly. I didn't see anyone, but I felt like I wasn't alone. "Hello there?"

Nothing.

"Hello?"

"Arlo?"

It wasn't my wife or daughter; yet, the voice sounded familiar. I walked into the grass and peeked around the back of the garage. No one.

"Who's there?"

"Arlo, it's me."

I shuffled carefully in the shadowy backyard while trying not to fall. Past Parker's basketball hoop that I helped Reggie attach to the side of the garage a few years back when Parker wanted to learn to play. Past a large plastic bench which stored random balls, plastic shovels, bottles of bubbles, and sidewalk chalk. Past Paige's motorized Barbie car. Past the trampoline that I was deathly afraid one of them would die on.

In the darkness, I hit something with my foot.

Jesus, I almost tumbled forward. I caught myself before falling over. *Just what I need right now.*

At first, I thought it was one of the kids' toys, so I stopped and looked around to see if whatever it was went flying. I didn't want to slip on the damn thing, whatever it was. Since I couldn't really see, I bent down and felt something soft. *Oh, no.* Instantly, I forgot about the woman's voice. I backed up a step and bent down, holding my cigar between my teeth. I didn't know how to work the flashlight on my cell phone, so I got out my lighter.

Banks.

Reggie's chubby, loveable gray cat. The one who liked to sunbathe on the porch. He was cool to the touch. I shook Banks slightly, but he didn't move.

Oh, no.

"Arlo?"

I looked up and saw her walking toward me. Quickly, I nudged a plastic bucket in front of Banks. Then, leaving him, I held my Montecristo between my fingers and took several steps forward. "Cora?" Confused, I asked, "What are you doing here?"

Cora wore a t-shirt shirt with a dark, button-down sweater over it, which she wrapped tightly around her torso. "I live here."

"So I hear. Which house?"

"Right there, two doors down," Cora answered, turning and pointing. "The stone one with the big garden."

I squinted. "Ah, I see." I really didn't. Like I said, it was dark. I puffed on my Montecristo. "Did you know this was my daughter's house?"

"Yes, I did. The day we met at the lake."

I paused. "You didn't tell me you were their neighbor?" It was a question, but I didn't know what answer I expected. But it was a question all the same.

"Arlo?" I heard my wife call from the house.

"Over here!" I yelled. Then to Cora, "My wife, Natasha."

"Ah..."

Natasha came toward us with a flashlight. "Over here," I said, waving to her.

"There you are, love," Natasha said when she reached us. "What are you doing out here? It's going to storm." She reached for my arm but then stopped.

"I just came out for a cigar," I said sheepishly then added, "This is Cora. We met a few days ago at the lake. Cora is Kate and Reggie's neighbor," I glanced at Cora, but she wasn't looking at me.

Natasha held the flashlight out in front of her and to the ground, so as not to blind any of us.

"Oh, hello, nice to meet you."

She extended her hand, and Cora took it, patting it gently with her other hand. "Very nice to meet you, Natasha. Arlo had very nice things to say about you."

Natasha rubbed my arm and smiled. "Well, he's the best."

There was an awkward moment of silence between the three of us, and then – just when I thought this sudden meeting couldn't get any more uncomfortable, it did.

"It looks like it's about to start raining any minute, Arlo. We should probably get going."

Cora abruptly took Natasha by the arm. "Wait!" she said, and then let go after Natasha jumped. "I'm sorry, I didn't mean to startle you just now. It's just that... well, I need to talk to Arlo."

"Excuse me..." Natasha retorted, obviously taken aback. She looked at Cora expectantly. "What exactly do you need to talk with my husband about?"

Cora wrapped her arms tightly around her middle again. She looked so small standing there in that oversized sweater. "I saw your SUV over here, and I thought this might be my only chance to talk to you. I really don't even know where to begin. It's about the book..."

"The book?" Natasha interrupted.

"Yes, the gardening book. Arlo, when I met you the other day at the lake, I had that book with me that my granddaughters bought me..."

"Oh, yes, I remember," I said. I bent down and put my cigar out in the grass then put the butt in my shirt pocket. "Kate has the same one."

Cora was visibly upset. "Right. Well, I got to thinking about that book. It goes over, in painstaking detail, several different types of plants and flowers. And in all honesty, you can see my garden. I have a beautiful garden... I only attempted to read it because the girls got it for me."

I laughed, because I understood what it was like to use something simply because it was from one of your grandchildren. Just like the picture frame that Parker made me out of popsicle sticks. No one would say it was a masterpiece. But I loved Parker, hence I loved the popsicle stick picture frame.

"Why would Kate have a book on gardening?" Natasha said, tapping a finger against her lips. "And I'm sorry, Cora, what does this have to do with, well... anything?"

Cora closed her eyes for several seconds and then took a

deep breath. She was obviously agitated, worried. "I'm sorry. This is hard for me. I'm not even sure how I want to say this..." Natasha and I looked at each other and then back at Cora.

"It's okay, Cora. Please... please go on," Natasha said.

From the house, I heard the screen door open. "Arlo? Natasha?"

"We'll be right in," I yelled to Reggie, then I turned my attention back to Cora. "My son-in-law."

"Yes. I know Reggie," Cora stated, barely above a whisper. "Okay. Here goes nothing. I thought the same thing as you, Natasha. Why the book? Kate doesn't do a lick of gardening. I think Reggie and the kids may have planted some flowers... anyway, sorry that's off track."

Natasha widened her eyes and looked from me to Cora. "Please, Cora. Go on, please." She was clearly getting annoyed. Her face said, *Did this woman have a point?*

"Okay. Around the time your granddaughter Paige got sick, Arlo, it was the same time my Charlie died. So, I didn't give it much thought. But later, after things settled down and I was in this big house all by myself, I started to wonder about the whole thing." Cora rotated her hands, making a spinning motion.

"The whole thing? You mean, with Paige?"

"Yes. You know, I always thought, and maybe at the time I was watching too many true crime documentaries, but I always thought, 'What if one of them did it?' Kate or Reggie, I mean."

"What the hell, Cora? You're accusing my daughter..."

Natasha grabbed my arm. "Arlo, let her finish."

I felt raindrops, a few on my arm and my forehead.

"Then I remembered the gardening book and wondered if there was some connection. I know it sounds strange." Cora stopped to catch her breath. Then the words came faster, as if she had to get it all out right then and there or she wouldn't have the courage. "There's lots of flowers that are poisonous to humans and cats in that book. There's an entire section on poisoning, what to do if a flower is accidentally ingested. Azaleas, hydrangeas, lilies, tulips... all poisonous."

"Stop right there," Natasha said. "Are you saying you think Paige and the cat ate *flowers*?"

"Yes, I am. That's exactly what I'm saying."

I felt a few more raindrops on my neck and face.

"But... it seems unlikely that Paige and Gibson would have accidentally eaten enough of any plant for it to be fatal. Or life-threatening, in Paige's case," said Natasha.

"Plus, Kate and Reggie don't have any flowers in their yard."

"Right," said Cora. "But I do. All of them."

I heard the screen door open again, and the porch light turned on. It was Kate this time who yelled out. "Dad?! Are you coming in? What are you guys doing out there? It's raining, for heaven's sake!"

"We're coming in, Kate. Just a minute."

The door slammed shut.

"My God," I mumbled under my breath. "Cora, you live two doors down. I could see Gibson wandering over there, but not Paige. Not without someone noticing, at least. She was three at the time."

"I know this is difficult for the two of you to hear, and I debated telling you, Arlo, or keeping my big mouth shut. But then I met you, and you were so kind and, well... I always had my suspicions. But when I finally put it all together..." Cora paused. I couldn't tell if she was crying or if it was the rain. "If it was one of my grandchildren, I'd want to know."

I was in shock. Could Kate or Reggie have poisoned my granddaughter? And if so, how?

And more importantly, why?

Still holding the flashlight, Natasha reached for Cora and gently took her by the shoulder. "We never thought it was an accident. Arlo and I, we never thought it was just an accident."

"But why, why would they do this?"

Natasha turned to look at me and let go of Cora. "No, not *they*. Arlo, love... her. *Kate*."

"What?"

"She... Kate did this."

I rubbed my hand down my face to wipe the raindrops away. "You can't really think that Kate poisoned Paige? And on purpose? Why, what would be the reason for it? This is nuts. I know you two don't get along, but poison her own child? No, I can't believe Kate would do that."

"Listen," Cora broke in. "I could be completely off base here. Maybe I shouldn't have said anything. Maybe I'm completely wrong. But still. I needed to say it."

Natasha took her glasses off and wiped them with her shirt. Her long hair was matted to the side of her face, and she pushed it back behind her shoulders. I looked at my wife, who had become so tiny, so fragile in what seemed like the blink of an eye.

"This can't be happening. For Christ's sake. This can't be real," I whispered.

And then I remembered Banks.

CHAPTER 41
ARLO

October 1, 2019 – Tuesday

"Can I have the flashlight?" I asked Natasha. She handed it over, and I added, "I have to show you two something."

It was raining harder, the Pennsylvania sky now littered with ominous clouds. The women followed close behind me. "Here, he's over here…"

Natasha asked who I was talking about, but I didn't bother to answer.

I found the cat. I bent down and looked up at Natasha and Cora. "It's Banks. He's dead. I just found him before you came over to talk to me, Cora."

Natasha and Cora crouched down beside me. Natasha used my shoulder for balance.

"Oh, no. Poor Reggie. He loves Banks," Natasha mumbled tearfully, running a hand down Banks' soft belly, now almost completely soaked from the rain.

I heard the screen door again, and all three of us looked up at each other.

"Arlo? Natasha?" It was Reggie again, and, it seemed, within seconds he was standing over us. "What's going on? Kate sent me to..."

We all stood up slowly. "I'm sorry, Reggie. I found him a few minutes ago." I pointed the flashlight down in Banks' direction.

Reggie bent down and picked Banks up, cradling the cat in his arms like a baby. Just like he'd done the day before with Baylor. The day before, that couldn't be... so much had happened since then.

"We're so sorry," Natasha said to Reggie, patting him uncertainly on the shoulder.

"Thank you. I... I don't know what's going on here," he responded, clearly dumbfounded. Then, as if suddenly realizing her presence, he questioned, "Cora, what are you doing here?"

Cora went to speak, but Natasha interrupted her. "She just stopped over to say hello."

"In the rain?"

"Yes, I saw Arlo and..."

"Reggie, I didn't know Cora was your neighbor."

"Yeah, I guess it never came up," Reggie said, preoccupied. He appeared lost in thought as he softly stroked Banks' neck.

Reggie was tall, taller than me by an inch or two. And, although he wasn't a large man or overly muscular, Reggie was strong, fit. I always saw Reggie as someone that wouldn't back down from a fight, if provoked. But right then, he seemed so small and vulnerable, holding Banks like he had with Parker and Paige when they were babies.

We all watched him for a moment, not really knowing what to do. Fortunately, it was Reggie who broke the silence, even if it was by reprimanding us. "You're going to get sick. All of you."

"You're probably right," Cora answered. She lingered for another moment. "Natasha, it was nice meeting you. I should be going. Goodnight, everyone." She stroked Banks' forehead a few times and then gave Reggie an awkward hug.

With that, Cora turned and briskly walked away, her soft, blonde hair stuck to the back of her head and neck. She turned around momentarily to yell back to us, "You better get going too. It's going to get really bad here soon."

I frowned, wondering if Cora meant the weather or something else.

Natasha asked, "Where's Kate?"
"She's putting Paige to bed. Come on in and at least say goodnight. You don't want to leave on a bad note."

My wife and I exchanged looks. "I think it's best we go."

"Arlo, no. Please. I know it's late, but Kate's having trouble getting Paige to bed. She's already pissed at me. And now Banks..." Reggie shook his head then closed his eyes for a beat.

"Reggie, do you think... I mean, what do you think happened to Banks? Just the other day you were holding Baylor and knocking on the garage door."

"I don't know. I just don't know."

Reggie turned back toward the house, but I gripped his shoulder with my good arm. "Come on, Reggie."

"What? What do you want me to say, Arlo?"

Natasha held out her arms. "Reggie, may I?" she asked, and Reggie handed the feline over to her. "I'll get something out of the car. We can bury Banks next to Baylor tomorrow."

Reggie nodded. "Thanks Natasha." Then, directing his attention back to me, said, "What do you want me to say, Arlo?" I handed Natasha the flashlight, and she walked away from us.

"I want you to say that Kate isn't capable of this."

"Like I said Arlo, I don't know. I mean, c'mon. Do you really think Kate could do this?"

I hesitated. "Reggie, the two of us should know Kate better than anyone. I mean, she's my daughter and I love her. But let's be honest. It's possible, right?"

Reggie squinted and nodded slowly a few times. "I know she's been under a lot of stress..."

"Celeste's death. That's what started it. And Paige's illness." I looked at Reggie and tried to figure out what he was thinking. "Postpartum depression, stress at work," I went on.

"Yeah..." Reggie had a distant look in his eyes.

"So can you really say Kate isn't capable of doing this?"

Reggie seemed to snap out of his fog. "What? No, I can't, Arlo. I can't say that."

The rain was steadily coming down now. My clothes were drenched, and I could feel the cigar, soaked and useless, in my shirt pocket.

"Do you think she's capable of hurting the kids?!" I screamed.

Reggie licked his lips and shook his head slowly then wiped raindrops away from his eyes. "How do I answer that, Arlo? How do I admit that my wife may have done this?"

CHAPTER 42
NATASHA

October 1, 2019 – Tuesday

I searched Arlo's bag in the back seat and found a sweatshirt I thought he might not miss. For having a lot of money, my husband sure didn't dress the part. It was something that, quite honestly, I loved about Arlo though, that humble, unassuming nature. Holding Banks with one arm, I spread the sweatshirt out across the backseat with the other. My hand started twitching again (it had started a few days earlier), which made this awful, arduous task that much more difficult.

In addition to being soaked, Banks was *heavy*. I noticed that my strength had diminished rather quickly in the past few weeks. I wasn't even the same person I was a month ago. Something I began worrying about recently was, *How much worse am I going to get?* How rapidly would my mind and body decline? Or, worse yet, would I merely deteriorate so painstakingly slowly that I became a burden for years and years to come?

I was selfish to marry a man so much older than me, knowing that I could (possibly, probably...) develop this horrific genetic disease. Knowing that his first wife died so young. And knowing that Arlo would be an old man trying to take care of me. It was so unfair to him.

After I set Banks down in the middle of Arlo's sweatshirt, I wrapped the sides and sleeves around him. The whole ordeal was depressing, knowing that Reggie loved Banks so much. Knowing that he named all of his cats after famous African American baseball players, in memory of his grandfather, who he adored dearly.

And knowing that Kate might have actually done this terrible act, that was the most frightening part about all of it. Because if she had poisoned Gibson three years ago, then she could have poisoned Baylor and Banks, too.

And she would have poisoned her daughter, either on purpose or accidentally.

From the other side of the yard, I heard Arlo yell for me, but I couldn't make out what he was saying. The rain was relentless, and then suddenly there was a deafening clap of thunder.

"What? Arlo?!" I shouted back, to no avail.

The back porch light was on, so after I finished with Banks and shut the car door, I headed over to the house. This was the last place I wanted to go, back into Kate's house. But what other choice did I have? I could have sat in the car with the dead cat, or, if the door was unlocked, I could have gone up to the loft above the garage. Neither seem like appealing options.

I walked through the sunporch and quietly called for Arlo. I definitely didn't want to feel the wrath of Kate if I were to wake up Parker or Paige. The kitchen light was off; the only light on was above the sink. I padded through the kitchen and peeked in the living room, which was off to my left. A few lamps were on. No sign of life. I backtracked and went into the dining room, where Kate was sitting alone. A single lamp was lit on the buffet table. Kate looked terrifying, like a woman scorned.

I wondered if, in another lifetime, we could have been friends. If the two of us could have gone shopping together and talked about our hobbies and ambitions and problems over chips and margaritas, like I did with Joyce.

But not in this life. No, Kate hated every ounce of me from the very beginning. Because I replaced her mother, even though Celeste had been gone for nearly two decades by then. She still resented me.

Kate was sipping what appeared to be whiskey from a rocks glass.

"The kids asleep?" I asked, leaning in the doorway.

Kate looked up, just realizing I was there, but not wanting to appear startled. She wouldn't dare give me the satisfaction. "Yeah, finally." She took a sip and set the glass back down on a coaster.

"We're going to... to be leaving. I just wanted to say goodnight."

Kate didn't look over at me, just stared at the table. Then she picked up her glass and downed the rest of the brown liquid inside. "Goodbye, Natasha."

I drummed my fingers on the wall. My hand felt sore from the small motion. I felt like I wanted to say something more, but then again, why waste my breath? I turned to walk away but stopped when Kate spoke again.

"Wait," Kate said. She stood and turned around, refilling her glass from a Bushmills bottle. Kate placed the bottle back down and turned to look directly at me. "I'm sorry you're sick, Natasha."

Kate took a long sip from her glass and almost completely finished it. She paused, looking down into the glass, then drank the rest of the whiskey. "I hope you get the help you need." She turned back toward the buffet.

I stood up straight and smiled. "I appreciate that. Thanks, Kate. Same to you."

Before she could question what I had said, I pivoted and walked through the kitchen. I found Arlo and Reggie talking quietly in the sunporch.

"Sorry to interrupt. Where were you guys?"

"Outside. We saw you come in," Arlo answered.

I was exhausted. "Can we please go, Arlo?"

"Sure thing. Should I say goodbye to Kate?" Arlo looked from Reggie to me.

"That's up to you," I answered, shrugging my shoulders.

Arlo nodded and kissed my forehead then walked out of the room.

"Reggie, I'm sorry again about Banks. And Baylor, too. I'll help Arlo bury him tomorrow if you want us to."

Reggie shook his head. "I'd like to do it. I'll stop over tomorrow after work if that's okay."

"Yes, that's not a problem," I stated. "We should be back from Arlo's doctor appointment before then."

A moment later, Arlo rejoined us. "I think you might have to help her up to bed," he said to Reggie.

"Oh, boy. She's still drinking?" Reggie asked, and Arlo

nodded. "Tomorrow will be a rough day for all of us." He chuckled, but it was a sad laugh.

Reggie gave me a hug and shook Arlo's hand. Arlo, not wanting to feel left out, was having none of that and pulled Reggie in for a hug too.

"I'll drive," I said, pulling the keys from my pocket. We scurried through the yard as quickly as we could while the rain poured down on us until we reached the car.

I drove slowly due to the heavy rain. The windshield wipers were moving so rapidly. They made that awful *swish chunk chunk* noise that made my skin crawl.

Arlo sat looking out the window into the darkness. He didn't speak, and I didn't force him. All I could think of was that look on Kate's face and poor Banks covered up tightly in the backseat.

"I used one of your sweatshirts to wrap up Banks."

Arlo didn't answer at first. I wasn't sure if he even heard me. "Hmm?" Arlo rolled down the window about halfway and threw something out.

"Banks, love. I used your sweatshirt. One of your Callan Collections ones. What did you throw out the window?"

Arlo turned and stared at me blankly. "Oh, right. Banks. Sure, no problem. Thanks for doing that," he said, patting me on the leg.

"Was that your cigar?"

"Hmm? Oh, yeah. It was soaked."

"You shouldn't have littered," I scolded.

He patted my leg again. "Yes, I know. I don't even know why I did that. I wasn't thinking, I guess. I love you, Natasha." He left his hand on my thigh. "You're so beautiful."

I placed my hand on top of his and squeezed it then returned my hand to the steering wheel. "I love you, too."

"Sweetheart?"

"Yeah?" My hand was throbbing.

"Do you think that Kate poisoned Paige? I mean, do you *really* think she could have done that, like Cora suggested?"

I thought for a minute, tightening my hands around the wheel. My left hand twitched again, so I stretched my fingers out slowly a few times inconspicuously.

"Oh, Arlo. Honestly, I..."

"Shit! Oh, shit!" Arlo shouted suddenly.

"What?! What is it?!" I yelled back, swerving and sliding in the rain. Thank God no one was coming toward us. "Arlo, what is it?!" I yelled, once I gained my composure.

"I forgot my wallet. I think I left it on the kitchen counter."

CHAPTER 43
ARLO

October 1, 2019 – Tuesday

"I'm so sorry, sweetheart." I implored, yet again. "If I didn't need my ID and insurance card for my appointment tomorrow..."

"Arlo, you said that already, like a hundred times!" Natasha replied, obviously still peeved. "It's fine, let's just hurry back. You can run in and grab your wallet. I'll wait in the car." Natasha had her hands tightly around the steering wheel and was leaning forward, her neck straining.

"Do you want me to drive?"

"Nonsense. We're only a few miles away. Plus, like I said to you earlier, I want to do what I can, as long as I can. One day, I might not be able to drive, if I live long enough."

I was taken aback by how directly my wife spoke about her disease and getting sick. I guess she had a lot more time to process the diagnosis than I had.

Natasha pulled into Kate and Reggie's driveway and cut the engine.

"I'll be quick," I said, kissing her on the cheek.

The storm had subsided a little, but it was still raining. I hurried through the yard over to the sunporch. Before I even opened the door, I heard yelling.

This wasn't going to be good.

I wondered if there was any way possible that I could slip into the kitchen, grab my wallet, and race out without Kate or Reggie seeing me.

No dice. I peered around into the kitchen, where Kate stood with her back to me. She was yelling at Reggie, who was in the living room. I did a quick inventory and noticed two small pairs of sockless feet, barely visible at the top of the staircase. This wasn't going to be easy.

Walking into the kitchen, I noticed broken glass on the floor.

"Screw you, Reggie! I don't give a rat's ass what you think anymore!"

I'd never seen my daughter this crazed before. Sure, I'd seen her fly off the handle a few times, but nothing like this. Nothing even close.

Reggie was a good ten or twelve feet from Kate, and obviously, he was trying to abate the situation. He saw me, and his eyes grew wide. Kate turned to look at me.

"Hey, now. What's going on here?" I said as calmly as I could muster.

"Is everything okay?" Reggie asked.

"I forgot my wallet, that's all. I think I left it on the counter here in the kitchen. I got it out to give the kids a few bucks for ice cream..."

"Well it's not fucking here!" Kate screeched. Her eyes were darting back and forth. Black smudges from what I guessed was mascara covered the sides of her face and under her eyes.

"Kate, hon, do you mind if I check on the kids? Say goodnight to them?" I started to move past her.

"Yes, I mind. It's late." Kate reached for me, but I moved quickly past her.

"Arlo, I think you should go," Reggie said, as I walked through the doorway. I saw a bottle of beer spilled on the carpet and, directly above it, a family photo with a cracked frame. The room reeked of beer. So apparently Kate was throwing things now. This was new.

"What if I take the kids with me?" I asked. "They could spend the night at our house."

Kate had too much to drink and was clearly incapable of being rational; yet, somehow managed to take a deep breath and respond as if she was sober and sane. "No, Dad. Please, just find your wallet and leave."

I walked past Reggie with my hands up to show my daughter that I wasn't a threat. "Kate, it seems as if there is a lot going on here. Maybe you two need to talk without Parker and Paige in the house."

Once I reached the bottom of the stairs, Paige ran down to me. At the last step, she leaped toward me. "Pappy!"

I was unable to catch Paige, so she kind of landed around my leg. There were tears in my granddaughter's eyes, which made my stomach churn. She wore Hello Kitty pajamas and smelled like strawberries.

"Hiya, Paige." I looked up to see Parker sitting on the top step. He had his hands wrapped around himself and was sitting up straight as an arrow, trying to appear unafraid, brave. "Parker, my boy. Why don't you help Paige and the two of you each pack a bag – underwear, clothes, your favorite stuffed animal..."

"I don't sleep with stuffies anymore, Pappy."

"Oh, okay. Well, one for Paige, then. You two will stay with me and Nooni tonight."

"Yay!" Paige yelped. "Pappy, Mommy is scaring me. She's yelling at daddy."

Reggie spoke up, "It's okay, sweetie. Mommy and Daddy are talking about some things. But it will be okay." He went to walk toward her, but I held up a hand and nodded reassuringly at my son-in-law. He stopped.

"It's okay, Paige," I said, squeezing her tightly toward me with my left arm. "Sometimes adults fight. But your mommy and daddy love you very much."

Kate, who had been pacing back and forth and drinking from a rocks glass, darted toward Paige and me. "The kids are staying here!" she yelled. "It's Reggie who will be leaving."

"You've got another thing coming if you think I'm leaving you alone in this house with our kids," Reggie said, surprisingly calm.

Suddenly, Kate threw her glass to her right. It hit the wall, brown liquid coloring the cream colored wall. The glass shattered into what seemed like hundreds of pieces. Kate simultaneously rushed toward Reggie while screaming, "You're nothing but a damn whore! Don't act like I don't know!" Kate flung herself at Reggie as she scratched and pawed at his head, his face, and chest.

Holy Christ. I'd never seen Kate like this.

I ushered Paige upstairs, and she did as she was told.

"Both of you, in your rooms. Pack!" I turned toward Kate and Reggie and saw Natasha appear in the doorway.

Eyes wide and no longer seeming sick or small, Natasha shouted, "What in the hell is going on here?!"

"Natasha, thank God," I answered. "Please, go upstairs and help the kids pack bags."

Kate turned and, seeing Natasha, completely forgot about Reggie. At least momentarily. She darted over to Natasha, who was on her way over to me. Kate got so close to Natasha's face their noses were almost touching.

"And you!" Kate screamed. "Couldn't find someone your own age?! You had to *waltz* into our lives, steal *my* dad!"

I attempted to position myself between them, while Reggie grabbed Kate by the shoulders and pulled her back a few steps.

Natasha was shaking with rage. "We know what you did, Kate! And I'm calling the police," she said, shaking her finger at Kate.

Oh no.

"Natasha, please!" I begged. "Not now..."

Abruptly, Kate calmed and stared at Natasha. Kate's facial expression gave nothing away. "The police? What are you talking about?"

"Don't act like we're idiots. We know what you did to Paige!"

"I don't know what you're rambling on about, Natasha. Reggie has been having an affair. For *years*!" She turned to look at Reggie, who at once let go of Kate's shoulders and stepped back.

"Kate..."

"Oh, come on, Reggie. *Tara.* I know about Josie's mom,

Tara." Kate was crying now. Natasha and I exchanged glances then focused on Reggie. *Oof.*

"That's what this is about?" I asked. "Reggie's having an affair?"

Reggie sighed deliberately, glancing at me. "Kate, can we please not talk about this right now?"

I spoke up. "Listen up, the both of you." Reggie and Kate turned to look at me. Tears streamed down Kate's face, and she was breathing heavily. She looked like a caged animal ready to pounce. It disturbed me to see my daughter this emotional. This... manic. I reached for Kate and wrapped my arm around her shoulder.

My poor Kate.

Reggie looked like he was on the verge of breaking down himself but clearly had more self-restraint. It suddenly crossed my mind, *how often does it get like this – this bad – between the two of them?*

I let go of Kate and turned to face her and Reggie. "Whatever is going on between you two, it's none of our business," I added, pointing upstairs. "But those two kids are my business. And you are scaring the shit out of them. Shame on you!" I turned and put my arm around my wife. "Natasha and I are taking them to our house. Someone can pick them up in the morning before –"

Kate interrupted, "Wait, what's this about the cops?! Natasha said she was going to call the police!"

Natasha looked at me, silently pleading with me. "I'll be upstairs with the kids," she said and snuck up the steps quickly.

I closed my eyes, preparing myself for how in the world I could even begin to...

"You! It was you, Kate!" Reggie howled, advancing toward her again. He squinted, pointing at her accusingly. "Banks is dead. Baylor, yesterday. You poisoned them! And Gibson too. That's what happened to Paige!"

I stepped toward them and attempted to grab Reggie by the arm, but he batted my hand away. "Reggie, please."

"You almost killed our daughter!" He yelled, ignoring me. "I mean, my God, she's scarred for the rest of her life because of you!"

"What?! Banks is dead? Baylor? No, I... I would never have done that! What is wrong with you, Reggie?!" Kate shook her head vigorously. "And what in the world would make you think I'd hurt Paige? Or the cats. That's just ludicrous!" Kate looked at me. "And you? You think this too?!"

I was at a loss. Did I think my daughter was capable of this? I wasn't sure. I longed to see that young girl, the one before all of the bad stuff happened. Kate was Paige's age when her mother died. How didn't I see how badly see had missed her mother? And, my God, how Kate looked like Celeste.

Kate's eyes darted from me to Reggie and back. "What type of person do you think I am?!"

I still couldn't respond. We all hesitated, the three of us in a small circle. The pain and anger and tension – all almost palpable in one another. I silently prayed that we were mistaken, that Cora was wrong. My daughter could not be capable of any of this, could she? I studied Kate and tried as hard as I could to see her as someone who wasn't my daughter. Was Kate capable of poisoning her husband's cats and, in turn, possibly poisoning her own daughter? My granddaughter?

Yes, I realized, she was.

I finally spoke. "Cora. Your neighbor. The book. You have the same book, on the bookshelf in the apartment."

Kate wiped her eyes. "What book?"

"On gardening. Something about the ins and outs of gardening. Flowers. It talks about what's poisonous to cats, to humans." I started to wonder if I sounded as ridiculous as I thought I did.

"I don't own a book on gardening. Have you seen our damn yard?" Kate reached for Reggie's arm and mine. "Wait, *Cora*... didn't her husband die around the time that Paige got sick?"

Reggie considered this for a few seconds. "I think so. But what's that have to do with anything?"

"I don't know!" Kate yelled. "Maybe she was angry with us. Maybe she put the book there. Like, to frame me."

Natasha came down the steps with the kids in line behind her. Both children looked at me but refused to give either one of their parents even the slightest glance. Once they reached the living room, Natasha ushered both children around her, wrapping an arm around each of them.

The three of them... they looked so natural, so innocent in that moment.

"Arlo, let's go. We're going... I'm taking the kids to the car."

Kate ignored Natasha. She looked up at the ceiling, thinking. "Yeah. In fact... Paige, sweetheart? Didn't you say you saw Mrs. Barnes in our yard earlier tonight before dinner?"

Paige buried her head in Natasha's side and hugged her tightly.

"No, no. She did! Paige said she saw her outside."

I crouched down beside Paige, that faint smell of strawberries breaking my heart for some reason. Nearly overcome by the surrealness of it all, I softly placed my hand on her back both for Paige's reassurance and mine. "Paige, is that true? Did you see Mrs. Barnes outside earlier tonight? Is that what you told Mommy?"

Natasha carefully patted Paige on the shoulder. "C'mon, babe. This is important."

"Tell them, Paige," Parker said, his voice breaking.

Paige twisted her little body and looked at me. "I told Mommy I saw Mrs. Barnes. I did! I did see her."

"See!" Kate yelped. "See, she must have done something to Banks."

We all exchanged looks. "I'm going to talk to her," Reggie said, searching for his shoes.

"I'll go with you."

"Fine," he said, finding a pair of sneakers in the kitchen. Reggie put them on while standing but leaning on the wall for support. "Let's go."

I hugged Natasha and asked, "Can you take the kids home? Can you drive?"

"No, they're fine!" Kate said, bending over to embrace Parker.

"We want to go to Nooni's," he said, shying away from his mother.

Natasha looked down at Kate. She treaded lightly with her words. "Kate, I think... maybe just for tonight, it would be for the best."

Kate seemed to finally give in. She smiled sleepily and nodded. "Oh, right," Kate said, getting to her feet. "Yes, of course. Especially if anything happens... with Mrs. Barnes."

Reggie hugged both kids tightly then turned to Kate. "Why don't you go relax?" he whispered to his wife. "We can talk about everything tomorrow, okay? Maybe when whatever this is settles down, we can go away for the weekend. Talk about everything."

Kate nodded, relenting. "Sure. Yeah, okay. Sure, Reggie. I'm going to take a bath and then... drift off." Kate kissed the kids softly on the top of the head. Parker winced but allowed his mother the satisfaction. Paige followed suit and hugged her mom.

Kate gave Reggie a long hug. Reggie was obviously surprised by this, but he let Kate in close and he kissed her cheek lightly.

"I love you all," she said, sighing heavily.

"We love you, too," Reggie said.

Kate then turned to me. "I'm exhausted, Dad. I'm so, so tired."

"Go get some rest, Kate," I said, pulling my daughter close and kissing the top of her head.

"And thanks, Natasha," Kate said, turning toward my wife. "Thank you for keeping the kids."

"Of course," she replied, once again embracing both Parker and Paige tightly, shielding them.

Kate hesitated then smiled softly. "Reggie will pick them up in the morning."

CHAPTER 44
ARLO

October 2, 2019 – Wednesday

The storm subsided, a light spattering of raindrops was all that remained. Reggie and I walked Natasha and the kids to the car. Parker no longer needed a booster seat due to his height. I still had a booster for Paige; although, she honestly was probably too tall for one. Reggie strapped Paige in and, after Natasha pulled out of the drive, we snapped our flashlights on, making our way down the drive.

My mind was going a mile a minute. I didn't know if my daughter was capable of hurting anyone, especially someone she loved. How had I been so blind to her obvious current state of, I don't know... distress? Hysteria?

And Cora? I barely knew the woman; yet, I couldn't believe that she had done these horrible things either. What would be the purpose?

"What are we going to say?" Reggie questioned me as we

walked through their backyard. "I mean, Arlo... I don't know what to think now."

Out of the corner of my eye, I could see Reggie looking at me. This was probably the first time I was ever mad at my son-in-law, rightfully so. "You're having an affair?" I said, coldly, in lieu of an answer.

"I thought you said it was none of your business?"

The grass was wet. Luckily, I had my boots on. But my shirt and jeans were still damp and sticking to my skin from the downpour earlier. I stopped and spun to face Reggie. "You're right, it's not. But I'm still pissed about it. Kate is still my daughter."

Reggie nodded. "I had a brief fling a few years ago. I ended it."

I started walking again then stopped to let Reggie lead the way. We made our way around the front of Cora's big stone house. An attractive wooden fence surrounded the yard. But since there was no gate, the only means to the house was around the front, unless we leaped over the fence and crushed Cora's greenery. Even in the dark, I could see the various trees and flowers that encased her backyard.

"And that's it?"

"That's it. I never told Kate about it, but apparently, she found out... somehow."

I didn't quite believe Reggie, but I didn't really have a reason not to. And, like he said, what happened behind closed doors wasn't really my business. Although I was not happy with him, what mattered most at that moment was what really happened to Paige.

Yet, I couldn't help myself.

"Reggie, why would Kate be this angry about something that happened a few years ago?"

We hesitated before walking up the steps to Cora's front porch.

Reggie clicked off his flashlight and shrugged. "I don't know; unless she just found out. Which is what must have happened."

"Who's the woman?" I asked, turning my flashlight off too and walking up the porch steps.

Reggie scratched his head and closed his eyes briefly. "Shit, Arlo. Honestly, just someone I met. A client's daughter. I made a terrible mistake."

It was shamefully late to be knocking on anyone's door, but Reggie did it anyway.

"And maybe you made more than one mistake?"

My son-in-law was safe from answering, at least for the time being. Cora opened the door pretty fast for someone who wasn't expecting company. Unless, of course, she was. Cora was wearing slippers but was otherwise still in regular clothes; although, she had changed out of her sweater from earlier. "I wondered if you'd be back," she said, stepping aside and ushering us in. "I realize this is a lot to take in," Cora added, shutting the door behind us.

"Want to have a seat in the den." It wasn't a question, and Reggie and I followed Cora through the dark hallway to a room on the far-left side of the house. Two floor lamps were dimly lit in opposite corners, giving the room a pleasing and somehow almost sensual feel.

Reggie and Cora both took a seat on the sofa, while I sat in one of the two wingback chairs opposite them. I studied the room while Reggie told Cora of the events that transpired. How all of this was happening, how and why we were confiding in this neighbor who was basically a stranger – especially when this stranger could have poisoned my granddaughter – was the most bizarre and nonsensical thing I had ever experienced. And I had watched my first wife die in front of our entire family.

Maybe I was worn out by the events of the past few hours, or I was still in shock from Natasha's diagnosis, but whatever it was, I was suddenly too tired, too drained to take in much else.

There was no television in the room; although, it was more of a study than a living room. An old wooden desk, which appeared to be both very heavy and very expensive, was positioned to my right. In front of me, built-in bookshelves were home to numerous paperbacks and small plants. I noted that I could see Kate and Reggie's garage and most of their backyard and driveway from the windows to the right of the bookshelves. I wondered how often Cora sat in this room and watched them and the other neighbors. I assumed plenty.

"Why in heaven's name would I have approached you or Arlo if I had anything to do with poisoning the cats or Paige?" Cora was saying to Reggie sincerely. "You want to call the cops? We can call the cops." Cora reached for her cell phone, which was on the coffee table in front of her.

"No, wait. We really don't even know if the cats were poisoned," Reggie inserted, lightly reaching for Cora's arm.

I finally spoke up. "Three cats in three years. Two of which died in two days, Reggie. That doesn't sound like an accident."

Cora glowered at me, disappointed. "I swear, I'm telling you both what I know to be true, that's it. Take it or leave it."

"I wish I'd had a necropsy done on Gibson back then. That would have solved everything."

I nodded in agreement. I had coaxed Kate and Reggie to do just that three years ago, but they'd naturally been so consumed with Paige that they didn't pursue Gibson's death further.

I was now beginning to wonder if Reggie was the cause of all of this; however, that really didn't make sense to me either.

"Were you in our yard earlier?" Reggie asked Cora. "Paige said she saw you in our backyard."

"I was. Parker and that other neighbor boy, umm... Miles, I think. They were kicking a ball around in the backyard, and it landed in my bushes. I just brought it back and put it near the... other stuff... in your yard."

"Oh, okay. Well, thanks, Cora. I'll tell Parker to be more careful."

Cora pursed her lips and gave a slight nod. "Well, lads. Unless you plan to call the cops on me, I have a busy day tomorrow..."

It was our cue to leave, and we took it as such. Cora walked us to the door, and I could hear her latch it as we descended the porch steps.

I was no closer to knowing the truth.

"Do you think we should call the police?" I asked Reggie as we traveled between the houses. The rain had almost completely stopped; only a slight sprinkle remained. I had no idea what time it was, but if I had to guess, I would have said it was the dead of night.

"No. I don't. Listen, Arlo, I wasn't completely honest with you before."

"Oh?" I responded, feigning shock.

I could really have gone for one of my Montecristos right about then.

"The woman I had the affair with, Tara. It was three years ago, and it started shortly before Paige's accident..."

"Shortly before?" I asked.

"Maybe six, eight weeks before."

We were now back in their yard, but the two of us stayed outside, on the driveway under Parker's basketball hoop. What I wouldn't have given for a cigar.

"I'm listening."

"I've been thinking about something, and I know this is going to sound so bad, but... shit, okay..."

I couldn't cross my arms because of the stupid cast, and I didn't have a beer, and I couldn't have a smoke because they were in my car and at home. And I was dog tired. "Get on with it, Reggie," I said, agitated.

"Tara and I started messing around again recently."

"Hmm. And just how recently?"

"I dunno. Couple of months, maybe. Anyway, what if Kate knew this whole time? What if Cora's right and Kate did poison Gibson and somehow, probably accidentally, also Paige – to spite me. To hurt me."

I considered this and nodded. "Well, if Kate did find out about the affair and knew it was happening again, I guess she could have killed Baylor and Banks to upset you."

"She knows I love those cats, that they were a way for me to remember my grandfather."

"Yeah. Yeah, that makes sense. Although, frankly, I can't imagine Kate doing any of this. She is my daughter, after all." I swallowed hard, trying not to imagine that Kate was capable of such horrible things.

"I understand. I've just been thinking about it."

"Reggie?"

"Yeah?"

"How the hell am I gonna get home?"

We both chuckled, which seemed immensely freeing and severely inappropriate at the same time.

"I'll drive you. Let me just go get my wallet and keys."

"I'm coming in too." I added, "I have to take a leak."

The house was the way we left it, with most of the lights off. Reggie searched the living room for his things, while I used the bathroom off of the kitchen. Then, I raided their fridge for a beer. Hell, I wasn't driving, and it had been a long night. To hell with my doctor's appointment. To hell with all of it.

Reggie walked into the kitchen, a funny look on his face.

I whispered, "Hey, you and Kate could use some space for each other. Why not instead of dropping me off, you just stay at my house? The kids are there, so you can just take them to school on your way to work... what's wrong?"

Reggie put his palms up and shrugged. "I can't find my keys.

"Could they be upstairs?"

"I guess. It's just that I always hang them on one of the hooks in the other room. But... okay, let me just gather up a few things and look upstairs for my keys. I'll leave Kate a note and text her in the morning. I don't want to wake her."

"God, no," I said, leaning against the counter and taking a long swig of Harp Lager. Who needed to be sober for a new cast, anyway?

Reggie quietly hurried up the stairs and down the hallway. I heard him open a door and within seconds I heard him holler, "Kate! Oh, God, no!"

CHAPTER 45
ARLO

October 2, 2019 – Wednesday

The bathtub was filled to the top – on the brink of spilling over. The water was red from what had to be my daughter's blood. Though at the time, I couldn't bring myself to comprehend this. Reggie was pulling Kate's limp, naked body out of the tub.

"Get me some towels!" he cried, and I quickly found some and threw them on the ground. Reggie wrapped Kate's body in one and applied pressure to her wrists. "Arlo, Arlo!" Reggie snapped his fingers, and I looked from Kate to him but couldn't form words.

"Arlo, I need you to call 9-1-1. Can you do that?" His voice was remarkably calm, paternal.

I nodded but didn't say anything.

Kate's long, damp hair was bunched around her, and I seemed to be able to focus on that for a moment. Reggie was still applying pressure to her wounds. "I need to start CPR. Arlo, call 9-1-1!"

Again, I just nodded, wasting precious time.

My poor, poor Kate.

Reggie clapped his hands together loudly, "For Christ's sake, Arlo! Snap the fuck out of it!"

Then I was dialing 9-1-1 and talking to what seemed to be a robot of a young man on the phone. I was giving him an address, I was giving him my name, Kate's name, Reggie's name. I was running down the steps and forgetting all about falling, and I was waiting outside for an ambulance.

I was leading a middle-aged woman and a young man up the stairs and standing in the hallway while they did what they could and tried to find a pulse and checked my daughter's vitals. Reggie was talking to the EMTs and using medical jargon I didn't understand.

I was in the way.

I didn't know whether or not I should call Natasha because it may wake the kids. I didn't have any cigars, so I busied myself with cleaning up the kids' rooms; although, I didn't know where a damn thing went, so I just put stuff anywhere. Just to keep moving, just to be productive.

Reggie was going with Kate in the ambulance. Suddenly, I was alone in their house. And, without a car or keys to their vehicles, I was trapped.

I'd have to call Natasha and Sean.

Not knowing what (if anything) Parker and Paige should know at this point, I called Sean first, clearly waking him up. I moved from Paige's room to the master bedroom, searching for car keys.

"Dad, is everything okay? It's nearly three a.m."

"No, no. It's not," I answered, now running purely on

adrenaline. I flicked the light on and began looking on top of the dressers. "It's Kate. She had an accident."

"Kate? What kind of accident?" Sean asked, groggily.

"She hurt herself. It's a long story, but Reggie's on his way to the hospital with her now."

No keys on the television or the bed.

"Okay, so let me get this straight. Kate had an accident, and Reggie is driving her to the hospital now. Is it bad?"

Nothing on top of the chest of drawers by the window.

"No, Reggie's isn't driving her. She's in an ambulance. She cut herself."

"Cut herself? Victor! Victor, get up. It's Kate. Dad, what hospital? Is she okay?"

Then, on the nightstand, I spotted them. Reggie's car keys. I knew they were his because of the Pittsburgh Pirates keychain.

"She slit her wrists, I think."

Sean gasped loudly. "Jesus Christ. Is she okay, Dad?"

"I don't know. I don't think so."

"Dad, are *you* all right?"

"I don't know…"

"Where are the kids and Natasha?"

"They're okay. They don't know yet. Natasha is with Parker and Paige at our house. Reggie and I found Kate. Natasha and the kids were already gone by then…"

"Victor and I are driving out. Tell us where to go."

Although I shouldn't have driven, I decided to drive myself to the hospital. I grabbed Reggie's keys. Underneath, a single white piece of lined paper was folded in half. The top read, "I'm sorry."

"Dad, are you there? Dad?!" Sean was shouting into the phone.

Tears formed in the corners of my eyes. "Sean, I found a note. Kate left a note."

CHAPTER 46
ARLO

October 2, 2019 – Wednesday

Those hours in the hospital waiting room were some of the longest of my life.

Reggie, Sean, and I sat silently for news. Reggie was the only one permitted to see Kate, and that was only once for a brief minute. Victor had been at the hospital but then went to my house to stay with Natasha and the kids. Victor updated Natasha, but we were all in agreement with Reggie that it was best to let him talk to the children when the time came. I busied myself with eating stale chips from the vending machine and smoking cigars outside (I had Sean stop at a convenience store and buy me a few cheap cigars). Since you weren't allowed to smoke near the building, I found myself walking the perimeter of the parking garage, counting my laps around until I'd lost track.

I must have walked a hundred miles.

I found myself thinking about Kate and where I'd gone wrong over the last three decades. I silently cursed Celeste (which I rarely did) for dying on me. If Celeste hadn't passed like she had – so unbelievably fast and so young – maybe Kate wouldn't have been so broken. I did what I could for her, but I also acknowledged then (and over and over again) that I wasn't the father she deserved. I was too wrapped up in surviving and forgetting and making money for my kids' future. I had no idea what my young daughter needed at the time.

It only further proved that money couldn't buy happiness.

I'd only felt helpless a handful of times in my life. When Kate had that allergic reaction as a child – that was scary. And when Celeste died and when my parents died. And when Paige was ill and went into a coma – that was one of the worst times of my life. I didn't know what to do when Natasha left me, and I didn't know why. And, of course, when Natasha returned and told me about her condition. I didn't know which was worse – her leaving or coming back ill.

But none of that trauma had prepared me for losing my daughter. No, this wasn't something I hadn't seen coming, even though I should have. The signs were all there, but I'd been too wrapped up in my own struggles to see Kate's pain for what it was.

I had failed all of the women in my life.

As I rounded the corner and snubbed out my cigar on the sidewalk, I could see the sun beginning to rise. Orange and yellow rays peeked out from the mountains in the distance. My God, I never tired of seeing that view.

CHAPTER 47
ARLO

July 4, 2020 – Saturday

Natasha was walking with a cane these days, but overall she was getting along rather well. We've spent a good chunk of money making the house handicap accessible by installing extra railings and two ramps. But no amount of money in the world mattered when it came to my wife's comfort and safety.

I suggested we move but Natasha insisted she liked the tranquility our rural area offered. And her occupational therapist, Thelma, advised that it was good for Natasha to take walks in the yard and toil in the garden when she was feeling up to it. And when she wasn't, Thelma told Natasha to sit on the deck and read and soak up the sun.

Independence Day was hot and unrelenting, with not a cloud in the sky. Reggie brought over Paige, Parker, and Parker's friend Miles, who were all playing kickball in the yard. I told Reggie to keep an eye out for any bobcats.

Naturally, Sean and Victor arrived early and with lots of

food and booze. It was the first holiday we celebrated as a family since Kate passed, and I reluctantly agreed that it was, in fact, one to actually commemorate.

Although, I was sad. I imagined I'd be sad for the rest of my days on Earth.

Joyce and her sister, Bonnie, as well as Reggie's mother were chatting with Natasha under a large pavilion we'd rented, in preparation for rain or extreme heat – it could have gone either way with our mountain weather. Bonnie's daughter, Hazel, played with the other children in the yard. Harvey brought his niece and nephew, so there were a good number of kids on hand.

I was happy to see Paige was able to keep up with the other kids – for the most part. At the beginning of the new year, Reggie finally agreed to get her set up with an occupational therapist. And Paige had a private tutor, who Natasha found, and I paid for. As far as we all knew, Paige didn't remember being in a coma when she was three or being as sick as she was, and Reggie decided that was for the best. But he agreed to discuss anything Paige wanted to know with her when she got older.

My younger sister, Faye, showed up and was busy chatting with Harvey. I noticed he hadn't taken his eyes off of Faye. Maybe my long-time bachelor friend was getting soft in his old age.

My other sister, Audrey, came to visit for a while and help Natasha out. Both of my sisters were widowed, and they loved Natasha. I'd converted our game room into a guest space, so I was guessing Audrey didn't plan on leaving any time soon. Now that her husband was gone, she said she would consider moving back up to the Poconos from South Carolina.

I debated on inviting Cora to our get-together, but in the end I decided it was best to put that friendship to rest.

Reggie remained in regular contact with Cora until spring when he and the kids moved into a smaller house on the other side of town. It was ten minutes closer to Natasha and me, so I was happy with that.

Natasha felt like, as depressing as the reason behind it was, she could finally be the loving, nurturing grandmother that she wanted to be. Natasha had never been able to have children of her own, but she vowed to be a great Nooni to Parker and Paige as long as she was able to. Reggie permitted us to take the kids to Niagara Falls in the spring, and it was the best trip we'd ever been on with Parker and Paige.

The only person missing at our home was my daughter – beautiful, intelligent, but troubled. Kate had left a note, which I had left unread at the time. It was only right that Reggie should have read it first. The hand-written letter was lengthy, honest, and the hardest thing I'd ever read. I knew Kate's words verbatim and played it over and over in my head, daily.

In her letter, Kate said it all began when her mother died, and Kate wasn't able to pick up the broken pieces at such a young age. She was scared and hurt and unbelievably sad. She didn't have any close female role models to turn to or identify with.

Then, even though it was years later, I destroyed Kate by replacing Celeste with a much younger woman. In essence, Kate felt that I replaced – then forgot about – her mother.

Kate couldn't believe that I would start dating someone that was almost the same age as her mother was when she died.

Kate blamed me for a lot of her problems – problems she couldn't seem to get past. Although Sean said that I wasn't to blame for any of it. He and I both lost Celeste too.

Kate went on to say that she found out about Reggie's affair with Tara. She secretly poisoned Gibson with an exuberant amount of crushed up azaleas, hydrangeas, and other toxic flowers from Cora's garden. She basically made this fatal concoction into a drink, which apparently Paige had gotten to also. Kate had admitted that, although Paige drinking the fruity-smelling, pink liquid was not deliberate, Kate took too many pills and fell asleep on the couch. Reggie had been at work and Parker at school; it had just been her and Paige in the house. Kate hadn't actually known for sure if Paige had drunk any of the concoction until she started to become sick. Naturally, Kate assumed that Paige had at that point.

Regardless, Kate had lived with the guilt ever since. That was why she continued to work at the school, so she could keep an eye on the kids – especially Paige. She'd become depressed, anxious, and eternally remorseful ever since. She knew that she destroyed Paige's chance at a perfectly normal life, whatever that may have been. Her frustration with Paige's shortcomings was really a frustration with herself and her perpetual guilt.

Kate had confided in her doctor, who prescribed her anxiety medication and recommended that she see a psychologist. He was concerned with what appeared to him to be bipolar symptoms. Kate refused to get a psychological evaluation. She didn't want to be labeled as with a disorder, especially when she was a nurse. *How would that look?* she'd said.

When Kate found out that Reggie was cheating again, she couldn't resist the urge to take it out on his beloved cats. Despite her guilt over what happened to Paige. That was the part I had trouble dealing with. Kate knew what had happened to Paige and that she was the cause of it. Yet she was willing to do the same thing again.

Kate admitted that she couldn't live with the pain any longer – the remorse, the sorrow, the shame. It was all too much.

Although Kate was never what you'd call a spiritual person, she said she needed to atone for her sins with the ultimate penance. That part got me every time.

If only I'd known.

For the first time in a long time, I sat on the porch and soaked up the sun and enjoyed watching the kids play. Being a good husband, father, and grandpa was all I aspired to be. It was all I need to be.

Natasha slowly walked up to the deck using the ramp, which we had installed on the other side of the steps. We joked that we weren't sure which one of us was less safe on the steps.

Natasha came up next to me, and I set my drink down on the deck.

"Come here, sweetheart," I said, and Natasha sat on my lap. She was thinner now than ever but still healthy. Still strong.

"Happy Birthday, love," she said, nuzzling my neck. "A big year for you, no?"

I gave my wife a gentle squeeze around her waist. "Yes. I suppose."

"Welcome to seventy, love."

Acknowledgments

I am forever indebted to my husband and best friend. Jeff, you have never been anything but encouraging, understanding, and kind. You are patient beyond belief. I am so grateful for you. I'm honored and so lucky to have you as my partner in crime and partner in life.

To my one and only daughter, Leah. You have truly humbled me. I soak up every second of our kitchen dancing, car singing, Barbie playing, ice cream eating, vacations, daily escapades, and general chaos. Life with you is an absolute adventure. What an honor it is for your dad and I to have this front row seat to your life. We love you beyond measure.

To my amazingly cool parents, Phyllis and Paul. You have always been so open-minded and have given me tons of great advice. Thank you for instilling in me your love of good music and what it means to be kind. I know I've had some wild ideas over these forty-four years, so thank you for your endless love and support.

Much appreciation to Andrea Honigmann, DVM for your expertise and assistance in answering my (what must have sounded bizarre) questions about cat poisoning.

Thank you to Julie Kramer for your insight into the fields of occupational and physical therapy. Your help was vital and greatly appreciated! And thank you to Mandy because helping you become a better writer has really helped me become a better writer in the process.

A special shout out to my dear friend and early reader, Christy Hiller. Thank you for your honest feedback and advice. And for all of the free books!

Thank you to fellow indie author, Jill Cullen, for all of your collaborating, editing, and friendship. It's a tough world out there; I'm glad we're in this journey together.

Much appreciation to Tracy Alaia at Feathers Artist Market and Gifts, Tonya Beatty at Bookends Bookstore & Homeschooling Resource Center LLC, Carolyn Domasky and Bob Topper at West Yough Shoppe, Kyle Churman and Lauren Shoemaker at Werner Books & Coffee, and Vanessa Ortiz at The Cracked Spine Buffalo LLC. Thank you all for carrying my books in your stores and for your support of local and independent authors.

Thanks to all of my indie author and artist friends that I've met on my writing journey. I appreciate and love all of the support, encouragement, networking, and laughter.

Lastly, but certainly not least, a huge thanks to those of you who have spent time reading my stories, writing reviews, giving me positive feedback, and telling others about my novels. I never thought that when I started writing my first book that I would publish it, let alone sell any.

When my husband and I went on our second date in 2007 (to Primanti Bros.), I asked him what he would do for a living if he could do anything. I won't tell you his response, but mine was to be a writer. All of these years later – I get to read, write, mentor, and interview amazing, interesting people – for a living. Getting to do what you love every single day... what on Earth could be better?

About the Author

Leslie Savisky lives in Southwestern Pennsylvania with her husband, daughter, and the family's two dogs. Leslie has an AAS degree in Criminal Justice and BA in Sociology, as well as an extensive background in the social service field.

Savisky is the author of *Other People's Words, Almost Too Late,* and *These Broken Pieces.* She is also a contributing writer for a local Pittsburgh newspaper and parent magazine, a substitute teacher, and student mentor.

Leslie can be reached at: LeslieSavisky@gmail.com

For more on Leslie Savisky's books, articles, podcast appearance, speaking engagements, and social media, find her at: linktr.ee/lesliesavisky

Photo courtesy of Stacey Louise Photography

HELPLINES

988 Suicide and Crisis Lifeline 988lifeline.org
Text: 988

Crisis Text Line
crisistextline.org
Text: HOME to 741–741

The Youthline
theyouthline.org
Call: 877-968-8491
Text: teen2teen to 839863

Samaritans USA
SamaritansUSA.org
Call: 800-273-TALK

Made in the USA
Columbia, SC
06 January 2025